The Quirks

AND THE
FREAKY
FIELD TRIP

Books by Erin Soderberg

The Quirks

WELCOME TO NORMAL

CIRCUS QUIRKUS

QUIRKALICIOUS BIRTHDAY

FREAKY FIELD TRIP

The Quirks

AND THE

ERIN SODERBERG

ILLUSTRATED BY COLIN JACK

BLOOMSBURY

NEW YORK LONDON OXFORD NEW DELHI SYDNEY

First published in the United States of America in November 2015
by Bloomsbury Children's Books
www.bloomsbury.com

Bloomsbury is a registered trademark of Bloomsbury Publishing Plc

For information about permission to reproduce selections from this book, write to
Permissions, Bloomsbury Children's Books, 1385 Broadway, New York, New York 10018
Bloomsbury books may be purchased for business or promotional use. For information on
bulk purchases please contact Macmillan Corporate and Premium Sales Department at
specialmarkets@macmillan.com

Library of Congress Cataloging-in-Publication Data
Soderberg, Erin.
The Quirks and the freaky field trip / by Erin Soderberg ; illustrations by Colin Jack.
pages   cm
Summary: The Quirks, a magical family living in Normal, Michigan, look forward to
Halloween and the arrival of Uncle Cork from Scotland.
ISBN 978-1-61963-668-2 (hardcover) • ISBN 978-1-61963-669-9 (e-book)
[1. Family life—Fiction. 2. Magic—Fiction. 3. Halloween—Fiction. 4. Uncles—Fiction.]
I. Jack, Colin, illustrator. II. Title.
PZ7.S685257Qj 2015   [Fic]—dc23   2014038770

Book design by John Candell
Typeset by Integra Software Services Pvt. Ltd.
Printed and bound in the U.S.A. by Thomson-Shore Inc., Dexter, Michigan
2 4 6 8 10 9 7 5 3 1

WARNING! This might look like a normal book, about normal people, in a normal place . . . But read on and prepare to meet THE QUIRKS!

For Brett Wright and Michael Bourret,
who have been a part of this Quirky family
from the beginning.

Also, for all the Quirky characters
in my own family, who make great
source material.

Table of Contents

The Quirks

AND THE

FREAKY FIELD TRIP

CHAPTER 1

Tricks and Treats

Have you ever noticed that as Halloween creeps closer, a mysterious kind of magic fills the air? Every autumn, when leaves tumble and gardens close up and turn brown, many strange and wonderful things come out of hiding: bumpy orange pumpkins with lush emerald leaves; sweet, stripy candy corn and gooey gummy treats; strange, spooky masks and furry gorilla suits.

Halloween is certainly a magnificent holiday. But there are few families who enjoy this season of tricks, treats, and magic more than the Quirks

1

of Normal, Michigan. Most of the time, the Quirks squished and poked and pleaded with their powers, wishing and hoping they might be able to keep their magical secrets hidden from the world. Because it can be hard to fit in when you feel so different from everyone around you.

But at Halloween, oddities are appreciated. Masks allow people to become someone else for a short time. Makeup can turn even the blandest, most boring person into something spectacularly grotesque. Costumes can trick you into thinking a person is very different from her ordinary self. Haunted houses make you wonder what strange things might be hiding just out of sight.

The Quirks cherished Halloween because it was a season for celebrating quirkiness.

But sometimes, combining the power of a family's Quirks with the mystery and wonder of Halloween does not turn out as well as one might hope. Sometimes, our most quirky selves don't want to hide . . . *especially* on the most magical of holidays.

CHAPTER 2

Underwear Monster

Finnegan Quirk was wearing nothing but underwear. Again.

"I think you should put on some clothes," said his sister Molly. "Throw on a pair of jeans, at least. Maybe a T-shirt? Uncle Cork hasn't visited since you were a baby, and nearly naked isn't the most normal way to introduce yourself."

"He's family! Besides, underpants are pretty much the same as pants," Finn announced. He danced around the living room, swinging his

3

legs from side to side. "They're just shorter. My legs look long and strong in undies."

Penelope, Molly's twin sister, giggled. "You're five, Finn. I hate to break it to you, but your legs look short in everything."

Finn looked down at his naked legs and roared, "I'm an underwear monster!" He sashayed around the living room, wiggling his arms as he bopped his tush against the side of the old armchair. "Maybe this will be my Halloween costume this year." He crashed onto the couch cushions and chomped on a piece of gum. "Anyway, I'm wearing my good underwear. Put them on fresh this morning, so they're clean and spiffy."

Molly groaned. "That is so gross. Way too much information, Finn."

"Oh, I s'pose now that you and Pen are ten, you're too old to chat about underwear?" Finn grinned. "It's my favorite subject! Also, toots and booby traps. Hey! Maybe we should set a few booby traps to welcome Uncle Cork?"

Penelope and Molly were both quick to shout "No!" at exactly the same time. Finn had only recently discovered how much fun booby traps could be, and his traps always spelled disaster. The last thing they needed was yet *another* disaster—the Quirks' house was already messy enough, even after a whole morning of cleaning.

The Quirk kids had spent the past several hours organizing their bedrooms. Now they'd turned their attention to helping their mom, Bree, tidy up the rest of the house. Considering the Quirk home was filled with people who had magic powers, their house was impressively messy. It was amazing what three kids, a scatterbrained mom, a sleepy grandfather, a teeny-tiny grandmother, and two strange and quirky pets could do to a house the family had only lived in for a few months. Though the Quirk house was chaotic, there was something about the comforting mess that also made it feel like home.

All the Quirks had grown used to the mess that surrounded them. But Molly, Pen, and Finn were trying to get the place ready for the houseguest who would be arriving at any minute. The kids' uncle Cork lived in Scotland, and he was coming to stay for a week. Grandpa Quill was driving Cork from the airport at that very moment.

5

The kids' faraway uncle had called a few days earlier to ask if he could come for a visit. Bree and her brother rarely spoke or saw each other, so she was quite nervous about his arrival. Uncle Cork had only met the Quirk kids once, briefly—and that was almost five long years ago. The kids were eager to get to know their uncle better since he sounded like a pretty fun guy from the stories their grandfather told.

Since the afternoon Cork had called and suggested a last-minute trip, Bree had been cleaning her nervous energy out. Now their house was as close to clean as any of the Quirks' houses had *ever* been. Molly wasn't sure why they had to tidy up so much for family. Family understood things like messes and strange habits and bad jokes, she thought. Surely Cork would forgive a bit of dust. But Bree had seemed on edge and irritable in the days leading up to her brother's visit, so the kids did as they were told without asking too many questions.

"Hey, sisters, I was wondering something . . ." Finn flopped around on the couch, fluffing up the cushions. He squeezed his skinny arm between

two pillows and pulled out a piece of chocolate that had been hiding there for who-knows-how-long. "Ooh, candy!" Finn pulled his gum out and replaced it with the chocolate. As soon as the gum was out of his mouth, Finn disappeared from view.

Much like other five-year-olds, Finn was bursting with quirks. One was his preference for wearing only underpants. Another was his love of potty jokes. But the other, more unusual thing about Finn was his see-through-ness. Like most of the other Quirks, Finn had a special, magic power that made him unique and rather unusual. He was invisible to almost everyone, unless he was chewing gum. *Almost* everyone ... but not his sister Molly.

*Un*like the rest of the Quirks, Molly had no magic of her own. Her power? She was immune to the rest of her family's magic. So she was the only person on earth who could see Finn *all* the time, even when she would really rather not. Molly's "Quirk" (if you could even call it that) came in handy from time to time, but her magic certainly wasn't as flashy as invisibility or the other family powers.

After a long moment, Finn opened his melty-chocolate mouth and continued his question. "Here's my wonder: What is Uncle Cork's Quirk? Do either of you know?'"

Molly and Penelope both shrugged. "Dunno," Pen said.

Molly was puzzled. "I don't think Mom's ever told us. Hey, Mom," she called loudly. Bree was listening to the Beatles in the kitchen while she cleaned. She had the music turned up very loud. Molly yelled again; then their mother poked her head into the living room. She was wearing rubber gloves and had her hair piled on top of her head inside a blue kerchief. In one hand, she brandished an old-fashioned feather duster. In the other, she held a filthy wet rag that looked like it deserved a prize for its dirt-gathering efforts.

Molly relieved her mother of the feather duster and began to swish it around the living room. Several live dust bunnies ran out from under the couch and hid behind a chair. "Mom, you've never told us what Uncle Cork's Quirk is."

Bree tilted her head and frowned. "Haven't I?"

The kids all waited expectantly for her to continue. She didn't.

Before they could press her for information, a loud squawk blasted outside. The horn on the Quirks' old van sounded like a goose choking on a rooster. Gramps thought the horn sounded like bagpipes—his favorite instrument—so he honked it whenever he thought he could get away with it. "Gramps is home!" Finn cried, racing toward the front door. "Uncle Cork is here!"

Molly, Penelope, and Bree all followed him toward the front porch. "Finn!" Bree shouted irritably, just as Finn opened the front door. "Grab a stick of gum, dear heart. Even if Uncle Cork can see you when you're invisible, we do have a rule about keeping your Quirk covered up in the neighborhood and at school, right? No magic outside the house, unless you simply can't help it."

Bree glanced at Penelope and smiled gently. Penelope often *couldn't* help it, and they all tried to be forgiving.

"Wait . . . ," said Molly. "Are you saying Cork can *see* Finn? Even when he's not chewing gum?"

Bree coughed. "Oh, well . . . yes? At least, I think he can. But, um, I guess I don't know for sure. I'm sure things have changed a lot since the last time we saw your uncle." She shifted her weight uncomfortably and wouldn't look Molly in the eye.

Molly couldn't believe it! Was it possible that someone besides herself could see Finn, even when he was invisible? She'd thought she was unique with her immunity—but maybe she *wasn't*. She couldn't wait to learn what Uncle Cork could do! She wondered, was her uncle a little like her? Did they share a Quirk? Molly was eager to find out.

"Gum's a-comin'!" Finn replied. He pulled a fresh stick of gum out of a package on the front hall table. In the next instant, he popped back into view for the others to see.

"Underwear, Finn?" Bree asked, closing her eyes. "Seriously? You're going out there to meet your uncle in underwear? The whole

11

neighborhood will see you. Besides, it's only sixty degrees. You'll freeze to death. Run back in and put on something a little more appropriate."

After Finn slinked back inside, releasing a full-body sigh on his way past, the Quirk girls stood side by side on the porch. Bree had one hand on each of their shoulders. The old van clunked and cooled and then, finally, the front passenger door popped open.

Out hopped Cork Quirk.

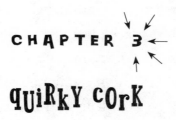

CHAPTER 3

QUIRKY CORK

"I haven't seen you girls since you were bitty!" Cork's Scottish accent was thick and fuzzy. It was as comfortable and familiar as a warm blanket that had been hiding behind the couch for months. "Come over here and give your old uncle a huggle!"

Penelope's eyes went wide as she took her uncle in. She remembered very few details from the last time they had seen him. And though they had a few pictures of Cork lying around the house, photos could *never* have prepared them for this.

Cork was average size, but that's where his ordinariness stopped. He was wearing trim yellow-and-brown-checkered pants with a pair of suspenders that looked just like the ones Grandpa Quill always wore. His shirt was blousy and white, with a floppy collar, and the sleeves were rolled all the way up under his armpits so it looked like he was wearing swimming floaties. His bushy hair was smashed down under a plaid newsboy cap and when he took it off, Molly and Penelope both gaped at the rainbow sweatband that wrapped around Cork's forehead.

Their uncle was a mishmash of styles, colors, and textures. The combination of his offbeat style and a huge, lopsided grin made it abundantly clear that Cork was going to be a very fun houseguest indeed.

"C'mon, now," Cork urged the girls with a smile. "I don' bite!"

Bree stepped timidly off the front porch and made her way over to her brother. She smiled nervously, and in the next instant, he picked her up and swung her around, laughing as he kissed her cheek with a noisy *mwah!* "It's good ta see you, Bree-tie."

Molly and Penelope both stared. Their mom had told them she wasn't close to her brother, but he obviously hadn't gotten that memo. Bree blushed and stepped backward. She used her polite, meeting-strangers-for-the-first-time voice to ask, "How was your trip? Did you get enough to eat on the airplane?"

"Fresh pineapple!" Cork declared joyously. "I charmed the stewardess and she brought me some of the first-class treats. Thought I was royalty, mos' likely! It's the accent. Works like a charm, it does."

Poof! Suddenly, a jeweled crown appeared out of thin air and teetered atop the rainbow sweatband and Cork's mop of tousled hair. An old-fashioned velvet cape appeared on his shoulders, and his left hand was wrapped around an enormous staff that had popped up out of nowhere.

15

Penelope gasped, but Cork simply chuckled and winked at her. "Ha! You picked up on the royalty comment, eh, Penelope?" He grinned. "I forgot how much fun we had playing around with your Quirk the last time I saw you girls! I'm lookin' forward to seeing what else you can do while I'm here this week."

Like Finn, Pen also had a special kind of magic power. The secret thoughts inside her mind sometimes came to life in an uncontrollable *poof!* There were times when her Quirk made it almost seem as if Pen's imagination was inside out. When she was nervous or anxious or when the world swirled and twirled around her in a crazy way, the visions inside Penelope's mind could become real. For the past several years, she had been working hard to try to control her Quirk, but sometimes she just couldn't stop her mind from wandering.

As Uncle Cork told them about his flight, Pen had pictured him as royalty and *bam!* Staff, cape, and crown. Penelope's eyes went wide, and then she closed them up tight. A moment later, the kingly attire disappeared just as quickly as it had come.

Cork placed his hat back atop his head. Then he cocked his head at Molly. She and Pen were both standing at the bottom of the porch stairs. "C'mon, girls, don't you remember me enough for a hug? I guess the last time I saw you, you were just wee high." He held his hand about a foot off the ground. "Now you're like beanstalks! Almost as tall as your mother."

Molly stepped forward. Penelope dropped back, hiding in her sister's shadow. "Welcome to Normal," Molly said. "We're really glad you're here."

Cork reached forward and ruffled Molly's hair. Her long, dark spiral curls fluffed up under his hand, making her head look a bit like an overgrown Chia pet. He said, "I'm so pleased I get to hang out with you girls again. It's been too long. Now"—Cork glanced around—"where's that little brother of yours? Off hidin', I suspect?"

As if on cue, Finn burst through the front door. Though he was still wearing nothing but underwear, he had accessorized his already unusual outfit with a pair of yellow rubber boots, a fuzzy winter hat, and a long mohair scarf wrapped gallantly around his neck.

"Lovely," muttered Bree, rolling her eyes. "What on earth will the neighbors say?"

"I don't suppose it matters what the neighbors say, now, does it?" Cork said stiffly, lifting his eyebrows. The girls watched as their mother narrowed her eyes at her brother. The reluctant smile that had been pasted on her face for the past few minutes faded. Bree, who was usually extra-friendly and warm to everyone, seemed quite chilly with her brother. It sometimes took her a while to feel comfortable around people, but it seemed strange that she would be nervous around her own brother.

"Hello, Uncle Cork!" Finn cried as he zoomed down the stairs.

Cork lifted Finn into the air and held him out at arm's length. Cork squinted, looking first behind one of Finn's ears, then the other. "There's something a bit different about you, kiddo."

"You can see me!" Finn announced.

"Is that it?" Cork asked. "Well, yes, indeed! Last time I visited, you'd gotten pretty blurry, kid."

Though Finn had been born magic-less, over the course of his first year, he began to fade. By the time his first birthday rolled around, Finn was totally transparent. It was only after the Quirks moved to Normal that Finn had discovered the one thing that made him visible for the entire world to see: chewing gum. The only other time Cork had come for a visit, Finn hadn't yet gone totally invisible, but he wasn't much more than a faint outline.

"It's great that the rest of the world can see you in full color again, young man," Cork said, setting Finn down. He gazed up at the Quirks' house, admiring their crumbling steps, wide front porch, and the white clapboard house that matched all the others in the neighborhood. "Where's Mum?" he wondered aloud.

Grandpa Quilliam Quirk, who had been awkwardly hauling Cork's suitcase from the back of the van, now tilted his head up and gestured toward the drooping willow tree. "We keep her house hanging up high in the tree here in Normal," Grandpa said. "She likes having a view of the neighborhood. She enjoys being so hidden up in the leaves."

"I hate that Mum has to hide," Cork grumbled, gazing around the neighborhood. "Jus' doesn't seem fair."

"It is what it is," Bree quipped back, her voice shaky. "You have your notions, and I have mine."

Before she and Cork could carry their debate any further, a tiny, birdlike creature came zooming out of the tree and nearly knocked Cork over. "My dear lad!" Gran Rose Quirk cried. "Look at'cha!"

Gran Quirk was another member of the family who was just a bit different from the rest of the world. Though she had no special powers, per se, she had been touched with a bit of Quirky magic. Gran wasn't born with her Quirk, but after she married Grandpa Quill, Gran had been cursed by her mother-in-law, who turned her from normal size to something that would fit inside a package of Easter Peeps. She was now a miniature, fairylike woman who also happened to be highly allergic to the indoors. Because of her allergy, Gran lived in a small house that the Quirks carried with them from town to town whenever they moved. She loved her little house, and enjoyed spending her days working among her vegetables, flowers, and herbs in the garden.

"Mum!" Cork shouted, sweeping his mother into his enormous hands. "You look like a peach."

Gran snuggled up against Cork's hand and kissed his thumb. "We've missed you so much, son. Can't you stay forever?"

"Don' I wish," Cork said. "But I need to head home in a week. 'Tis what it is." He headed up onto the front porch and settled in on the large swing. Finn cuddled up next to him, while Molly and Penelope perched on the front rail nearby. Gran and Grandpa Quirk both gazed lovingly at Cork. It was obvious he'd been greatly missed since the last time they'd seen him. Missed by everyone except Bree, that is, who still looked very uncomfortable and out of sorts. "Don' want to overstay my welcome. Booked my flight back for the day after Halloween. Figured this was a great time to come for a quick visit, since I know Halloween is Dad's favorite holiday over here in America."

"True," Grandpa Quill said. "Masks, ghosts, and spooks are all good fun—it's great to see what people choose as their disguise for a day. Besides, any excuse to eat a lot of candy makes for a mighty fine holiday."

Cork strode over to the edge of the porch and dug into his enormous suitcase. "I'm sure you'll be expecting that I brought pressies for everyone? Good news! I do have a few special things from the homeland."

"Me first!" Finn begged. "I love presents! My sisters just had their birthday party, so they don't need any more. I can take them all off your hands for you, Uncle."

Cork laughed loudly. "Okay, kid, fair enough." He rustled around in his bag and pulled out a thin, rectangular box. "I think you'll have some fun with this one."

Finn ripped the box open and pulled out a pair of plastic glasses. He tried to read the tag. He had only been in kindergarten for a few weeks, and was still struggling to correctly identify all the letters

in the alphabet. "*Ex rye nye get vi*—I give up! Can someone read it to me?"

Cork perched the glasses on the end of Finn's small nose. "These are ultrasonic, super-bionic, X-ray, night-vision goggles. So you can keep an eye on shenanigans during Halloween." He winked at Bree and tipped his hat at her. "It's always good to keep an extra eye on things, don't you think?"

Bree looked away and said nothing. Molly and Penelope looked from Cork to Bree and back again. Cork continued unloading presents from his suitcase—special candy for Bree; an oddly colored, dried chunk of meat for Grandpa Quill; fancy Scottish yarn (that smelled a little too much like *actual* sheep for Pen's taste) for Gran to knit with. He'd also brought books and sweets and really chunky wool sweaters for all three kids, and a cowhide coin purse that Finn eagerly snatched up. It was a wonder Cork had any room for his own things inside the bag.

23

As Molly watched her uncle, unloading one strange gift after another, she wondered once again what her uncle's Quirk might be—and when he might reveal it. Her mother's gift was the power of persuasion—she could make people think or do whatever she wanted them to do (though her power was limited to controlling only two or three people at a time). Perhaps Cork had a similar power?

But no, Molly thought, what would that have to do with him being able to see Finn? And anyway, she and Penelope and Finn were all very different, so siblings obviously didn't automatically have similar Quirks. Several times over the years, Molly, Finn, and Penelope had figured out how to make their Quirks work together, but there was no denying that they were all very different people with very different magic.

Once again, Molly wondered if maybe Uncle Cork was more like her. What if he didn't have a Quirk? Maybe, just *maybe*, Molly thought, Cork was Quirk-free! Perhaps that would explain why Grandpa Quill and their mom and Gran had never talked about his powers—he didn't *have* any magic!

Molly observed her uncle Cork laughing and lavishing gifts and stomping around the front porch. He was odd, entertaining, and delightfully unusual. Cork was a real character, that was for sure. Which meant—magic or not—he was most certainly a Quirk.

CHAPTER 4

Gramparone

Dinner Was served on the back deck later that night. It was chilly, but they all wanted Gran to be a part of their family reunion and she never came inside—even to eat. So everyone bundled up and Bree brought a space heater to the deck. They wrapped themselves in blankets and ate dinner picnic-style.

25

"So Dad tells me you've been in Normal for a few months," Cork said, looking at Bree. "How's it going so far? Think you'll stick it out a bit longer?"

Penelope glanced at her mother. Bree shrugged and politely said, "Things seem to be going pretty well, actually. We've had a couple of exciting adventures." She looked at the kids, who grinned.

In fact, the Quirks had had *quite* a few adventures in the months since they'd moved to Normal. First, they'd had to settle in at school. Penelope's magic meant fourth grade was often very interesting. Then there had been Normal Night, the town's annual celebration. After he'd discovered his gum trick, Finn had started kindergarten. And just a few weeks ago, the Quirk kids had gotten to be a part of the circus that had come to town. They were making friends, settling in, and enjoying school. Even Bree had met some new friends— she was becoming buddies with other waitresses at work, and had also been spending some time with the girls' fourth-grade teacher, Mr. Call-Me-George Intihar.

"You'll be happy to hear that for the first time in a while, we've gotten to know one of our neighbors," Grandpa Quill said. They all glanced over at Mrs. DeVille's house next door. Mrs. DeVille was a crabby older woman who'd recently made friends with Gran, despite Gran's rather unusual size. Mrs. DeVille was willing to look past Gran's differences, which was a refreshing surprise. For the past few weeks, Mrs. DeVille had been joining Gran and Gramps for tea on the deck most afternoons. That night, however, she was nowhere to be seen. "Things are going mighty fine, so far. This is town number twenty-seven for this crew, so we're hoping this move will last for a bit before we have to hit the road again."

"Twenty-seven towns?" Cork's eyebrows shot up. He looked at Bree and shook his head, only slightly. "Not really?"

Molly nodded. "Really. Every time we start to get comfy somewhere—"

"Someone's magic gets us in trouble and we move before anyone figures out our secrets," Penelope finished. "More often than not, it's my fault. But I've been working on controlling my Quirk these last few months, and it's starting to work! Molly's been helping me."

27

Cork smiled. "Tha's wonderful, Penelope. I'm proud of yeh. Of course, I'm proud of your magic, too. Don' get me wrong about that."

"Watch this," Pen said. She looked at the plate that had been filled with cookies just a few minutes earlier. As she focused on the plate, Pen closed her eyes, squeezed her lips together, and hummed. Several of the crumbs that were left on the plate scooted closer and closer together, then—*poof!*—they joined into one small chocolate chip cookie in the center of the plate. Penelope's eyes flew open, she reached out her hand, and popped the cookie into her mouth. "Voilà! I was thinking about how a little more dessert would be nice, and then I made it happen."

Grandpa Quill rubbed his belly and said, "That's one way to do it." He smiled and burped and Molly knew he was probably thinking about how many times he used his own Quirk to get extra dessert. Grandpa Quill's power was that he could rewind time, which meant he could give himself a do-over when he needed one. If something bad happened—or something especially *good* that warranted repeating—Grandpa would just zip time backward and relive those moments or hours again. His powers had gotten a bit weaker with age, and when he used his Quirk too often he got very sleepy. But many nights he liked to rewind their dessert course a few times so he could eat his cake or ice cream or pudding a second or third time over.

"Uncle Cork, do you know how to control your Quirk yet?" Finn asked. "I do. I'm better at controlling my Quirk than Penelope, even. See?" He popped a piece of gum into his mouth, then pulled it out again. In, out, in, out. Finn zoomed into and out of focus. He was showing off.

"Whoa, kiddo, you're makin' me dizzy!" Cork cried. He shook his head and closed his eyes.

"Can you do that?" Finn asked again. "Make your Quirk go and not go and go and not go and—"

Bree pressed her fingers against Finn's mouth to make him quiet down. "I'm sure your uncle Cork is tired after his journey. Let's not interrogate him immediately. He certainly doesn't need to bring out his Quirk for the whole world to see first thing." She raised her eyebrows at Cork, and Molly saw a look pass between them that she didn't understand.

"It's not interrogation," Molly argued. "We're just asking a few questions. We want to know about his magic!"

"Maybe I don't have any magic," Cork said, winking at Molly. "Maybe I'm Quirk-less."

Molly perked up. "Really?"

"Enough now," Bree said quickly, cutting her brother off before he could say anything more. "If Cork doesn't want to talk about Quirks, let's leave him alone. No need to flash it all around. I think we all can understand his desire for privacy. Maybe now simply isn't the best time for us to discuss it."

If it was privacy he was after, Molly and Penelope most certainly *did* understand. After all, they'd spent the better part of the last five years trying to hide their family's magic from class-mates, neighbors, and twenty-seven different mail carriers. Molly didn't want to force her uncle Cork to talk about his differences if he wasn't comfortable discussing them. She'd learned from her experience with Penelope that people had to feel comfortable with and confident about their own differences before they could feel comfortable airing their Quirks in front of others.

"Tell me about school," Cork said, changing the subject away from the family magic. "What are you kids learning right now?"

"The fourth graders are going on a field trip at the end of this week," Pen said, after Finn had finished talking about the kindergarten's lessons on counting and saying sorry. "We're taking a bus to a pop-up museum!"

"Pop-Tart?" Cork looked confused.

Molly laughed. "No, pop-*up*. It's a temporary museum that's just popped up for Halloween. It's in an old party-supply warehouse in Durban, the next town over, and it's only open for a week. It pops up, then it gets put away again until next year."

"It's called Spook City," Penelope added. "We're going to learn about special effects and costuming and other cool stuff like that."

Grandpa Quill burped loudly again. He excused himself and said, "I'm joining the girls on the class trip. I'll be the Gramparone. That's my special term for a chaperone who is also a grandpa. I figure if I spend some time at Spook City with the kids from Normal Elementary, I might get some bonus ideas for costumes and decorations for the house on Halloween night. We'll see if this year I can scare a few people out of their wits when they come to the door and try to steal my candy."

Bree swatted his arm. "It's not *your* candy, Dad. When you're manning the door on Halloween night, you're supposed to give the candy to children. Not try to scare them away so you can eat it all yourself."

"I'm willing to share the candy with kids, but when a fifty-year-old man comes to the door and hollers 'trick or treat' in my face, I have every right to try to scare the guy, don't you think?"

Gran giggled. "The kid you scared away last year was a fifth grader, Quilliam. He was not a grown man. You made the kid cry, and he was with his friends. I seem to remember feeling bad for that boy."

"Well, he *looked* like a man," Grandpa Quill insisted. "He had a beard and everything."

"It was his costume! He was dressed as Abe Lincoln," Gran pointed out.

Grandpa Quill grumbled, "How was I supposed to know that? I just thought it was some big guy who was trying to steal all the candy from the children . . . and from me."

Penelope laughed. "Well, hopefully you'll learn a few things about costuming when we go to Spook City for the field trip, so you won't make that mistake again. While we're there, we're going to learn about how they design costumes for zombies and witches. And Mr. Intihar said there might be makeup artists who will show us how they paint faces for horror movies."

Finn's eyes got wide. He thrust his lower lip out and said, "I want to go!"

"You're not old enough yet. Our school doesn't do field trips in kindergarten," Molly reminded him. Ever since the girls had told Finn about their upcoming field trip, he'd been sulking. He didn't like the injustice of it—kindergartners never got to do anything, he claimed, and he was furious.

"I'm never old enough," Finn said.

"You're the perfect age for trick-or-treating," Molly pointed out.

"Too true," agreed Cork. "What kind of costume are you planning to wear for Halloween, kiddo?"

"Still deciding," Finn said, pulling his gum out of his mouth. "Underwear monster. Or a Star Wars guy. Or maybe the Invisible Boy."

"How about you and me team up?" Cork suggested.

Finn looked at him strangely. "Team up? You're old. That's kind of weird. Adults don't wear costumes."

"I'm thirty-two! And adults most certainly *do* wear costumes. Boring adults might not admit that they like to dress up, but the fact is, most everyone enjoys pretending to be someone else from time to time." He glanced at Bree.

Finn considered his uncle's suggestion. "I have an idea. I'll let you be my costume partner if you'll help figure out a way for me to get onto that bus for the fourth-grade field trip."

Cork shook his head. "No deal. I don't want your mum to kick me out. I jus' got here!"

"Then you're not my costume buddy."

"Fair enough." Cork turned to Penelope and asked, "Are you going to dress up for Halloween this year?"

Pen nodded. "I haven't decided what I'm going to be yet, though. I have to come up with something good so I get a lot of candy when we're out trick-or-treating. Some of our friends at school told us about one block in Normal that gives out full-size candy bars. Can you believe it? Big ones!"

"America . . . ," Cork muttered, gazing around the backyard. "Home of free, full-size candy bars." He grinned. "This is going to be quite a week. But folks, I'm afraid I must be off to bed. It's late, late, late in Scotland, and my body's not adjusted yet. If someone can point me in the direction of a couch or a spare patch of floor, I'd be a happy man."

36

Finn leaped up. "You get to sleep in my room this week, Uncle Cork. I'll give you my bed and my pillow. I'm going to sleep with my cars and LEGOs in a sleeping bag on the floor. Like camping! Oh, wait. Unless you want the LEGO bed I made, Uncle? You can take a look and decide, okay? Follow me."

Cork stood up and stretched. "Well, g'night all. It sure is wonderful to be back with the family again." Before he turned to head inside, Cork glanced over at the privacy fence that stretched tall between the Quirks' yard and Mrs. DeVille's house. Mrs. DeVille's curtains were all closed up tight, her yard seemed empty, and it appeared that she too had gone to bed for the night. But as he stared at the fence between the two yards, Cork yelled out, "Good night, neighbor! 'Twould be lovely to meet you face-to-face tomorrow sometime."

Suddenly, Mrs. DeVille's eye appeared, blinking through the hole in the fence. She'd been eavesdropping! The snooping wasn't unusual, but it was strange that Cork had noticed she was hidden back there. Usually, one of the Quirk kids spotted her when she was spying.

37

"Welcome to Normal, kid. I've heard a whole lot about you from your ma," called Mrs. DeVille.

"All good things, I hope!" Cork tipped his hat at their neighbor, then followed Finn inside.

In the silence that followed, Molly and Pen shared a look. "How did he know Mrs. DeVille was over there?" Molly whispered.

Pen shrugged. Neither Bree nor Grandpa Quill said anything. Gran flew up and over the fence to bid Mrs. DeVille good night.

"How *did* he know she was over there?" Molly asked again. "It's like he could hear her breathing or something. Is that his Quirk? Does Uncle Cork have supersonic hearing?"

Grandpa Quill ignored her. "I'd best head inside and get started on the dishes."

"Mom?" Molly asked. "Did you know Mrs. DeVille was back there behind the fence before Cork said something?"

"Good night, girls," Bree said in response. "It's time for you to mind your own business and get off to bed. You've got a big week coming up, and I don't want either of you getting sick." Then she, too, went inside, leaving Molly and Penelope alone outside to wonder without any answers.

38

CHAPTER 5

spook style

"Listen up, class!" Mr. Intihar clapped for attention. "I want to go over the details for the field trip Friday. We have some important things to prepare for before we get to Spook City, and I think you'll all want a few days to get ready for the fun they have in store for you."

All the fourth graders put their math workbooks into their desks and gathered near the back corner of the classroom. Mr. Intihar had recently brought in a few beanbag chairs to make their room feel more comfy, and several boys in the class were fighting over whose turn it was in the good seats.

"Nolan! Raade!" Mr. Intihar snapped. "Neither of you may use the beanbags. And Nolan, hats off. It's not Halloween yet, so no costumes." He glanced around the room. After a quick scan of the class, he pointed to Amelia. "Amelia, excellent work today. You may take one of the beanbag seats. And . . ."

Penelope held her breath, wishing and hoping that he would choose her. She hadn't yet had a turn in the beanbag chairs, and she longed for one. Much of the time, Penelope faded into the background at school. She liked it that way, since it helped make her Quirk less problematic. But it also meant she often wasn't noticed when Mr. Intihar needed to pick students for special privileges.

Today, however, Mr. Intihar's finger came to rest when it was pointing straight at Penelope. It appeared to be stuck. Mr. Intihar looked surprised for a moment, but still his finger wouldn't stray from Penelope. "And Penelope," he said, finally. "You may take the other beanbag chair."

Pen flopped down and got comfy, while Mr. Intihar investigated his finger. He stared at it and wiggled it and tried to figure out why it had felt like it had been *stuck* just a few seconds before. Finally, he cleared his throat and said, "I assume you all remember the most important field trip rules for later this week. Stay together, be courteous and kind, and listen carefully when the museum staff is talking."

"Yes, Mr. I.," said Nolan. "Ears open, mouths closed."

"Exactly, Mr. Paulson. Now, I got a call from the museum staff this morning. They've asked me to split you into two groups for our tour through the museum. They also wanted me to pass along some information about a challenge you'll all be taking part in while we're at Spook City."

"Guys versus girls?" Nolan shouted.

Mr. Intihar cleared his throat. "Remember rule number three, Nolan? Listen carefully."

"You said we're supposed to listen carefully when the *museum* staff is talking," Nolan pointed out.

"You are *always* supposed to listen to me. I know you're excited about the trip, but we need to get through the rest of this week first. And I would also appreciate good listening ears while I tell you about the challenge."

Penelope and Molly both glanced at Nolan. Molly noticed that Nolan's ears had begun to grow. They were nearly double the size they had been just a moment before. Hard as she tried, Penelope just couldn't keep her magic from acting up around Nolan. Their loudmouthed classmate grated on her nerves and set her mind spiraling

nearly every day. She did her best to avoid him, but Nolan was so outspoken and braggy in their classroom that it tended to be challenging to ignore him completely.

Mr. Intihar continued. "The museum staff will work with each fourth-grade team on a Spook Style team challenge. After each group gets a tour of the museum, you'll be working with some of the employees to design your very own real-life spooky monster or creature. You'll have the opportunity to use their special-effects makeup, costumes, and expertise to create the most realistic and *scary* creation you can."

"We're making monsters?" Stella blurted out. Then she covered her mouth and muttered, "Sorry."

Mr. Intihar gave her a weary look. "I don't know exactly how the challenge will work, but yes, you'll be designing monsters. Now, let me announce the teams so you'll know which of your classmates you'll be working with at the museum. We have two chaperones joining us, and I'll float between the two groups to ensure everyone is behaving appropriately." He pulled a piece of paper off his desk and read names off a list. "The first group will be with Mr. Quirk, Penelope and Molly's grandfather. This group will be Penelope, Joey, Amelia, Norah, Nolan . . ."

Penelope scarcely listened as their teacher read the rest of the names on the list. She was paired with Nolan? This would be a nightmare. At least she also had a few friends on her team, too. Penelope tuned in again as Mr. Intihar continued to list off names. ". . . Izzy, Raade, Stella, and Molly. The second group I called out will be with Stella's mom, Heather."

Wait. Penelope had a momentary flash of panic. "Did you say Molly is in the second group?" she asked quietly.

"Yes," Mr. Intihar said. "Molly's in the second group. You're in the first."

Penelope gulped.

Mr. Initihar went on. "The Spook Style team challenge will be judged by the museum staff. I thought it would be fun for all of you to spend a few days thinking about what kind of monster you might like to create with your group during the competition. Use the next few days for brainstorming and sketching, and then on Friday, you'll be ready to rock."

As everyone packed up to leave for the day, Penelope couldn't stop dwelling on the fact that she and Molly would be separated for the challenge at Spook City.

"You okay?" Molly poked her head around Pen's backpack.

"Yeah. It's fine. I'll be fine." Penelope didn't sound entirely convinced.

"Pen," Molly said quietly. "You *will* be okay. We've been in Normal long enough now that you've done a good job figuring out how to handle your Quirk without me."

45

"I know!" Pen blurted. "I said I'll be fine, Molly."

Molly put her hands up. "Okay, okay. You look a little sick about it is all."

Pen zipped her backpack closed and smirked. "I just feel bad you're going to lose."

"Excuse me?"

Pen lifted one eyebrow. "Your team is going down."

"Oh, is that how it's going to be?" Molly put her hands on her hips and grinned. "You versus me?"

"It's either focus on my team's win, or spend the whole day at Spook City worrying about my magic flaring up," Pen said. "Frankly, I'd rather enjoy myself on the field trip. As much as I love teaming up with you, I'm going to make the most of what I've got."

"I have to admit that with an imagination like yours on the other team, I'm kinda worried." Molly smiled widely and wrapped her arm around Pen's shoulders as they walked out the front doors of the school. "But I'm not letting my team go down without a fight. If you want to make this a battle of Quirk versus Quirk, I'm game."

"Monster versus monster, Quirk versus Quirk." Pen laughed and switched over to a TV announcer voice. "An epic battle will take place at Spook City on the field trip Friday. Tune in to see who will win!"

CHAPTER 6

Crazy Ed's Creations

"So what's good here?" Cork studied the menu at Crazy Ed's later that night. Since Bree worked as a waitress at the diner-style restaurant, the Quirks got to eat for free one night every week. The kids were excited to take their uncle on a fun outing to one of their favorite places in town.

"I always get the special," Grandpa Quill said, leaning back into the curved corner booth. "Don't care what it is. I trust Martha to make my stomach happy. Too bad for you, you missed lasagna night—that's Sundays."

Cork folded his menu closed and gazed toward the wall that separated the main dining room from the kitchen. He appeared to be carefully studying the paintings hanging there. A moment later, he patted the table and said, "I'm a trusting man. I'll risk the special. It looks good."

"You don't even know what it is yet," Molly pointed out. "What if you don't like it?"

"I have a feeling I'll love it." Cork grinned. He reached up to adjust his hat. Then he pulled it off and set it beside him in the booth. "'Tis rude to wear a hat at the dinner table, isn't it?"

"I think your hat is just fine," Bree snapped, glancing up at him over her menu. "You can keep it on. We don't have any rules about hats at Crazy Ed's."

"I've noticed you actually do have a lot of rules around here," Cork snapped back. "You want me to leave it on, is that it?" He started to put his hat on again, then reconsidered and set it back on the bench seat.

Molly didn't remind her uncle or her mom that Cork was still wearing his silly rainbow sweatband. Maybe that didn't count as a hat? Perhaps he considered it more of an accessory, like a headband or a scarf. She'd noticed he wore his sweatband at breakfast each morning, even when he'd come downstairs wearing nothing but a pair of fuzzy sheep pajamas.

Since he had arrived, the Quirk kids had been enjoying getting to know their uncle. He played with them in the backyard, took them for double scoops of ice cream in town after dinner, and played card games with Gran and Gramps on the deck late into the night. The only person who didn't seem to be enjoying his company much was Bree—and the girls still hadn't figured out why their mom was so unlike herself around her brother. She always seemed nervous and uncomfortable—and even a little crabby. It wasn't like her to be grumpy, ever!

"Finn," Penelope said, trying to prevent her brother from sneaking off to the dessert case. "I have an idea of how you can be a part of our field trip, even though you don't get to come along to Spook City. Mr. Intihar told us at school today that we're going to get to design our very own monsters or creepy characters at the museum. Do you want to help me come up with some ideas?"

"Monster design is my favorite." Finn leaped into the booth and pulled a pen out of his mom's apron. "I have a ton of ideas."

"Penelope and I are on separate teams," Molly told the others. She began to giggle and added, "Pen's on a team with Nolan."

Pen frowned. "It's not funny." She lowered her voice to a whisper. "You know how he makes my Quirk go crazy."

The bell that hung on the front door of Crazy Ed's jingled as Molly said, "Mr. Intihar was probably smart to split us up onto separate teams, since we really do make a pretty good pair."

"Did I hear someone say I'm smart?" All the Quirks whipped around as Mr. Intihar strode through Crazy Ed's and made his way toward their table. "Can't say I disagree! Hello, girls. Heidy-ho, other Quirks."

"George," Bree said, patting her hair. "Would you like to join us? This is my brother, Cork. He's in town, visiting for a week from Scotland."

Cork stood up to shake Mr. Intihar's hand. "Pleased to meet'cha."

"Likewise," Mr. Intihar said, his gargantuan smile spread wide across his face. "I didn't realize Bree had a brother. It's a real treat to have you here in town."

Cork continued to shake his hand, until finally Mr. Intihar pulled away. "You're a popular man, I hear. My nieces tell me you're taking them on a field trip on Friday."

"That I am." Mr. Intihar settled into the booth. "Now, this is a long shot, but I don't suppose you're free Friday, are you?"

Cork blinked. "I was going to do some knitting. Maybe stop in here at Ed's for a slice of pie and a bit of a chat with Bree. But other than that, I'm free as a sheep on a Sunday."

"See, I got a call from my other chaperone this afternoon. She's come down with a bug, and isn't going to be able to join us at Spook City. If we could get your paperwork through in time, is there any chance you'd be willing to come along and help me keep an eye on half a class of kids?"

"I'd love to do that!" Cork yelped. Many of the other restaurant patrons turned to stare. "I volunteer with a school group in my neighborhood back home—help with reading and some of their holiday craft projects when they need it. I also help the teachers by keeping an extra eye on their classrooms now and again, when they're doing small group work and things like that."

Mr. Intihar smiled. "Sounds like you're a perfect fit."

"You'll be in charge of my group, Uncle Cork," Molly said. "Gramps is assigned to Pen's team."

Finn hung his head sadly. "So now *everyone* is going to Spook City? This just keeps getting worse and worser."

"*I'm* not going," Bree reminded him. "I have to work. And you, young man, have school. Our obligations are a necessary part of life."

"Oblatations are the pits." Finn crossed his arms. He brightened a moment later when he remembered he was supposed to be helping Pen come up with ideas for the Spook Style challenge. He began to sketch some of his favorite comic book monsters and creeps on one of the Crazy Ed's napkins while the others chatted and ate. He used ketchup to make it look like his creatures were oozing blood.

Molly and Pen sat on either side of him, watching as their brother drew grotesque-looking slime monsters, furry beasts, and tiny critters with mouths full of teeth. The sketches filled the napkin as Finn sketched. At one point, a small scene began to play out on the napkin. It was almost like a little comic strip come to life. Monsters danced and fought beside the drawing of Crazy Ed's restaurant on the napkin. One of the slimy guys slithered off the napkin and slid onto the table, leaving a trail of green goo behind it.

Penelope slammed her eyes closed and hummed to clear the visions from her mind. "The field trip is going to be interesting," she noted quietly while

the adults talked and drank coffee on the other side of the table. "I was feeling okay about it all earlier, but now I'm starting to wonder if this is a good idea. How am I supposed to keep my mind from wandering with so many crazy things to see at a Halloween museum?"

"You just focus on not letting your thoughts run too wild," Molly said. "You can do that, right?"

Pen shrugged. "I hope so."

Cork leaned over to peek at Finn's drawings. "Those are pretty good, kiddo."

"Thanks, Uncle Cork. I like drawing."

"Your mum drew a lot when she was little, too. She was quite an artist."

"Mom draws?" Finn asked.

"You bet," Cork said.

"What else did Mom like to do when she was a kid?" Penelope asked. Their mom didn't talk about her childhood that much. They were always so busy getting settled into new towns and looking toward the future that it seemed she hardly had time to remember much of the past. "Were you two close?"

"When I was a wee little one, yeah," Cork said. "But as we got older, your mum and I drifted apart.

Had different ideas about our lives and such. 'Twas sometimes tough for us to get along."

Molly glanced over at her mom, who was deep in conversation with Mr. Intihar. Bree was a very private person, and she suspected she wouldn't appreciate Cork telling them much more about herself than they already knew. Still, she asked, "What kinds of different ideas?"

"Well . . ." Cork lowered his voice. It was as though he was preparing to share a secret with the kids. "For one thing, in the town where I live—"

"What are you all talking about?" Bree asked, interrupting their conversation. She looked nervously from Cork to Molly to Pen.

Cork looked at her briefly, then focused his eyes down on the tabletop. "Aw, it's nothin'. Kids and I are just chatting," he said. He winked at Molly secretively, and she hoped that meant this wouldn't be the end of their conversation. But it was soon clear that would be all he'd say about it that night.

After a silence that stretched on for far too long, Cork shook his head and asked, "So. What's for dessert?"

CHAPTER 7

Family Differences

Later that night, Cork's snoring was once again so loud that the walls of their house were practically shaking. After the first night of sleeping in the same room with their uncle, Finn had set up a small nest made of blankets and a sleeping bag in the hall just outside his bedroom. He fell asleep with his head covered in pillows, trying to drown out the sound. By the third night, Finn had convinced his mom to let him set up a small, cozy sleep nook in the attic. Finn loved the attic, and had been looking for an excuse to create a fort up there.

In the girls' bedroom, both of the family pets were curled into the farthest corner under Penelope's bed to escape the noise. Pen peeked under the bed and whispered, "Hi, guys."

Penelope's monster, Niblet, had his huge body wrapped protectively around Pickles, the family's newest pet. Though Pickles had started out as a rescue puppy—a Pomapoo—from the animal shelter, after a few minutes in the Quirk house, she'd turned into a dat. A dat was the Quirks' word for a dog who acted and looked quite a lot like a cat. Penelope had really wanted a kitten— so when they'd gotten a puppy instead, her imagination had turned their new dog into the perfect compromise.

"Pickles, come on out and play," Molly cooed. Pickles wriggled out of Niblet's arms and squirmed out from under the bed. She purred and rubbed her fluffy body up against Molly's arm, then barked to get Molly to throw her squeaky chicken.

While Pen cuddled with Niblet and Molly goofed around with Pickles, the girls got down to business. "Why do you think Mom's so weird with Uncle Cork?" Molly asked, voicing aloud the thing

58

she'd been dwelling over in her mind since the day their uncle had arrived.

"Mom is so strange around him! She's usually so friendly with everyone, so I don't get why she's awkward with her own brother," Pen said. "Do you think something happened between them?"

"I don't know. I am getting the impression Mom's mad at him or something," Molly said, tossing Pickles's chicken across the room. She watched the little puffball leap across their bedroom to retrieve it. "But I think we need to try to figure out how to make them be close, like Cork said they were when they were little kids."

Penelope rubbed Niblet's furry armpits. The monster giggled and rolled onto his back for a belly rub. "Cork is so much fun. I hate that we never get to see him. I would love for him to come and visit more often. Or for us to go to Scotland to visit *him*! Wouldn't that be fun?"

"So fun," Molly agreed.

"I like that he doesn't treat us like kids," Penelope said after a long moment. "And I'm glad he's coming along on the field trip. I just wish he was in my group."

"You get Gramps, though. That might be a good thing, considering you also have Nolan."

Pen leaned up against her bed and stretched her legs out into the center of the room. "What do you think Cork's Quirk is? Aren't you dying of curiosity?" Ever since he'd arrived in Normal, Cork had been coy about his Quirk, refusing to tell them anything about his magic.

"Yes! I think he's just keeping it a secret for funsies." Molly tossed the rubber chicken across the room one more time, then pulled Pickles onto her lap for a cuddle. "You do think he has a Quirk, don't you?"

Penelope gasped. "Oh! Do you think he could be more like you?"

"I doubt it. I think the only reason I don't have one is because of you. While we were cooking in Mom's tummy, you got all the magic, and I got all the good looks."

"Molly! We look exactly the same."

"I know." Molly smiled.

"We should get to sleep," Pen said, after her sister caught her yawn. "We could probably guess forever and still not figure out what Cork's Quirk is. Eventually I bet we'll get some clue that will help us figure it out." She yawned again. "Have you thought much about your monster design for the contest on Friday?"

"Not really," Molly confessed. "I'm hoping we'll get some good ideas when we get to the museum. I'm trying to leave my mind open to suggestions."

"I should probably do the same thing, but when I leave my mind open to suggestion, it can get a little messy." Pen giggled. "Right now, I've got Finn's monster designs printed all over inside my brain. I'm trying to focus on *not* focusing on them. We don't need any more monsters here." Niblet's tummy grumbled in response. Penelope pulled him in close against her body. "I love you, Nibbly."

Molly pulled her pajamas on and set out her clothes for the next day. Pen did the same, then each girl crawled into her bed—Molly up top, and Pen down below. Penelope liked being squeezed between her sister on the upper bunk and Niblet hidden below her bed.

Their mom came into the girls' room and whispered, "Lights out, girls." She padded over to Penelope's bed and bent down to give her a kiss.

Then she climbed up the ladder to Molly's bunk and leaned in to give her a kiss, too. For the past few nights, Bree's shifts had ended long after bedtime and the girls hadn't seen much of her in the evenings. Both Molly and Pen loved when their mom was around to tuck them in and snuggle for a moment before they fell asleep. It was their chance to talk with her and share their worries that had crept up throughout the day.

"Good night, Mom," Penelope said.

"I love you girls very much, do you know that?" Bree asked. She often asked them this, and it was always reassuring—even though they really *did* know just how much their mother loved them. She always protected them, and shielded the family from trouble, and she was comforting and supportive whenever they needed her to be. Often, Bree was a bit scatterbrained, but when it came to her kids, she was ninety-nine percent perfect.

"We do, Mom," said Molly. She flipped over onto her side and looked at her mom in the crooked light from the streetlamp outside. "Mom? Why don't you like Uncle Cork very much? You're kind of weird around him."

Cork's snores rumbled through the house as Bree considered her question. "I do like him," she said finally. "He's my brother, and there's nothing that can shatter the bond of family. But Cork and I—" She broke off.

"You have different ideas about your lives?" Penelope asked.

"Who told you that?" Bree wondered.

"Cork," said Molly. "But I don't really know what that means."

"Well, he's not wrong," said Bree. "I do love your uncle, very much. But he and I are very different, so sometimes it's hard for me to feel close to him."

Penelope pulled her legs against her chest. "But Molly and I are different—*very* different—and we still get along. Most of the time, anyway."

Bree sighed. "And I hope it will always stay that way." She patted Pen's leg, then stood up. "A lot of time has passed since Cork and I have been close. It's strange being with him again. Hopefully we'll get to know each other again someday, but for now, I'm doing the best I can. That's all I can do . . . try my best to understand him, and I hope he feels the same."

"I hope you get to be buddies again, too," said Molly. "Because we really like him. We like having him around, and it would be fun for him to visit more often. Or maybe we could go see him in Scotland sometime? I bet Gran and Gramps would love to go back to Ireland and Scotland sometime, wouldn't they? And you, too?"

Bree smiled faintly. It wasn't her usual, whole-body, sunshiny smile that made her radiate happiness. But at least it was something. "Good night, girls. Have a wonderful day at school tomorrow."

"Good night," echoed both girls.

After their mom had left, Molly whispered, "Sleep tight, Pen."

"You too, Molly."

There was a long pause, then Molly muttered, "We'll always get along, right?"

"I hope so." Penelope began to draw circles with her toe on the bottom of Molly's upper bunk. "Maybe we should make a promise? Just in case?"

"I promise," Molly said.

Pen nodded. "I promise, too. I love you, sister."

"Love you, too. Always, no matter what." Molly peeked over the edge of her bunk at her twin.

"Even if your Spook Style team crushes mine in the challenge."

"We'll try to crush gently." Pen giggled. "Now, good night."

CHAPTER 8

Birds for Breakfast

On the morning of the field trip—the day before Halloween—Molly woke to the sound of birdsong. Cheeping, chittering, and fluttering noises filled her bedroom. She peeked out from under her pillow and stifled a scream. A small, live, purple bird was perched on the edge of her bunk rail—staring at her. Molly slid her body back so she was pressed against the wall. That tiny bit of movement made the bird lift its wings and flap away.

"Pen?"

"Uh-huh?"

Molly whispered, "There is a bird in our room."

"Birds," Pen said. "Plural."

"You know about the bird? *Birds?*" Molly shrieked. She looked over the edge of her bed. There was Penelope, sitting in front of their dresser mirror, her hair held up by four fluttering birds. "There are *birds* in your hair!"

"They're the little guys from *Cinderella*," Penelope explained.

"That's a reasonable explanation?"

"Somewhat," Pen said. "I'm testing out my Halloween costume finalists."

"And the birds are . . ."

"Well, when I began to consider Cinderella as a possibility, they just appeared to help me design a costume. Like they did for Cinderella in the story, when it was time for her to go to the ball. The birds and mice helped her with her dress and hair and everything."

Molly yelped. "Are there also *mice* in our room?"

"Nope. Just the birds." She giggled. "For now."

Molly climbed out of bed and watched her sister from a distance. Pen was wearing a dress that looked almost exactly like the dress in the

Cinderella movie, and the birds were braiding her hair with their beaks.

"That's super-creepy," Molly said. With its beak, one of the birds lifted Molly's T-shirt off the pile of clothes she'd laid out the night before. It fluttered over to her and draped the shirt across her shoulders. Molly muttered, "Thanks. Pen, did Mom buy you that dress, or did you just . . . create it?"

"I imagined it. It seems like my mind's working overtime this morning. Between the field trip and Finn's monster sketches and Halloween coming up and Cork's visit, I'm a little overwhelmed."

Molly closed her eyes and sighed. "Awesome." She could already see that this was going to be an interesting day.

* * *

When the bus dropped the Quirk kids off at school a while later, Mr. Intihar and some of the other fourth-grade students were already gathered near the twisty slide on the playground. The fourth graders didn't need to report to their classroom that day. Mr. Intihar had told them it would be easier to meet outside, so they would be ready to load into the bus as soon as it rolled up.

Cork and Grandpa Quill were driving the Quirks' van directly to the museum. Finn had spent all morning begging them to let him join them. His begging had set both Niblet and Pickles into a frenzy, then that got Penelope's bird friends all worked up, and before long the house was a squawking, whining, sniffling nightmare. The birds disappeared shortly after Pen got some breakfast in her tummy, but Niblet, Pickles, and Finn were loud and yippy all morning.

"Molly! Pen!" Stella Anderson waved both girls over to where she was standing with a few of their other classmates.

Molly turned to say good-bye to her brother, but he was already gone. She'd thought he might have lingered awhile, trying to convince someone to let him come along, but it looked like he'd finally resigned himself to staying at school for the day.

Pen and Molly ambled over to their friends. Stella was yammering away. "I'm hoping to get some good ideas for Halloween costumes while we're at the museum," she was saying. "I want to be really scary for trick-or-treating this year. They're doing a contest at the community center on Halloween night, and the best costume wins a gift certificate for Crazy Ed's. My mom said if I win it, I can use the whole thing for desserts if I want."

Norah sighed dreamily. "Crazy Ed's has the best desserts."

"But nothing can beat the block that gives out full-size candy bars to trick-or-treaters," Joey Pahula blurted out. "That block is the best place to go on Halloween night, for sure."

As their friends chatted about Halloween in Normal, Molly noticed that Pen had retreated to the outside of their circle. "What's up?" she asked. Penelope was usually shier than Molly, but she'd started to loosen up in Normal. It was one of the things Molly liked best about their newest town—it had helped to pull Pen out of her shell a little bit.

"It's just . . . Halloween," Pen said. "There's so much *imagination* that goes along with this holiday, and I'll be curious to see how my mind handles it all."

"We're in fourth grade," Molly reminded her. "There's imagination everywhere, every day. You've

been doing just fine, so what difference will a few costumes and a little bit of makeup make?"

"You're right." Pen smiled. "Remember that time I tried to go to the haunted house? When we lived in Colorado?"

Molly laughed. She did remember. Penelope had so been freaked out about what kinds of creatures might be hiding, waiting to pop out from hidden nooks and crannies, that her mind had turned on all the lights in the haunted house.

All the other people who were there had moaned and complained and forced the managers to give them their money back. No one had any idea Penelope had been behind the technical difficulties, thank goodness, but Pen hadn't been back to any kind of haunted house since.

As Molly and Penelope rejoined the conversation with their classmates, the bus came rumbling around the corner. "Time to load up!" Mr. Intihar announced when the door wheezed open.

The fourth graders cheered. Everyone jostled to be first in line. Mr. Intihar called out names, making sure everyone was there, then he waved them all onto the bus. Molly and Penelope were swept up in the crowd and up the bus steps.

As Molly settled into her seat beside Norah, she leaned over the seat behind them to grin at Izzy and Stella. Penelope was across the aisle, sitting with Joey. Even though it was only their class going, the small bus was packed almost full.

"Leave the backseat empty," Mr. Intihar yelled to Nolan and Raade. "Trouble always starts in the back of the bus, so everyone can sit forward today."

Nolan groaned, and reluctantly took the only other empty seat—right next to Mr. Intihar.

The bus door sighed closed, and they all cheered again. They were off! Molly and Norah both got on their knees and leaned over the back of their seat again to talk to the friends behind them. When they did, Molly saw something that made her stomach flip: *Finn*!

Molly's mouth hung open. She stared at her brother, who was lounging across the very back seat of the bus. He was clearly invisible to everyone else on board, and it was too late to get him off the bus without making a scene. Molly's eyes narrowed, and she stared at her brother until he saw her.

He stuck out his tongue and waved. Molly sunk back into her seat again. She was very glum. She had been looking forward to the field trip for days. And now her enthusiasm had just hit a pothole. Because the fourth graders were on their way to Spook City . . . but so was Invisible Finn.

CHAPTER 9

Stowaway

There was a lot of pushing and shoving to get off the bus when they arrived at the museum. Mr. Intihar looked like he'd already had it with the class, and Molly didn't know how she was going to break it to their teacher that they had a stowaway.

Molly waited while everyone else got off the bus, then she grabbed her brother's arm. "This way, bucko."

"Ouch," Finn said, pulling his arm away. "Don't tug."

"How could you, Finn?" Molly demanded in an urgent whisper. She continued to pull him down the aisle of the empty bus. She held her backpack in the same hand so that it would just look like she was pulling that, instead of an invisible kid.

Molly dragged Finn down the steps. "I'm sorry!" Finn whispered, prompting Molly to shush him. "I brought my X-ray glasses that Uncle Cork got me so I can see behind all the walls and figure out the museum's secrets. I'll share them with you if you promise not to tell on me."

"Argh!" Molly groaned. Finn had done many naughty things in his life, but this was the worst yet. This time his actions would have a real impact on others—not just pranks, or tricks, or silly games he liked to play in the house. Sneaking onto a field trip bus was something far worse than any of those things. This time Finn had gone too far.

"Welcome, Normal fourth graders!" A tall woman with long, straight, black-purple hair waved her arm toward Mr. Intihar's students. She was dressed in a flowing skirt with a close-fitting top, and she had a string of chunky beads around her neck. Molly squinted to get a better look at the necklace . . . then realized they weren't beads at all, but tiny skulls. The woman was striking and beautiful—but also a little bit scary-looking. Molly noticed Penelope had turned away. She probably thought the woman looked a bit like a witch, and would want to squelch that thought before anything happened. "I'm Christine. I'll be working with one of your class groups today."

"I hope I'm not in Christine's group," Finn whispered. He and Molly were standing at the very back of the crowd, far enough from others that Finn wouldn't accidentally bump into anyone. "Sheesh, she's kind of creepy."

"You aren't going to be in any groups," Molly whispered out the side of her mouth. Mr. Intihar turned to quiet her. She smiled at him innocently.

When the purple-haired woman moved around, Molly noticed that it looked almost as if she were floating. Christine continued. "If you'll all follow me inside the museum—" Without smiling, she trailed off toward the museum doors. All the kids followed her at a distance.

Just as they reached the front door, Molly spotted the Quirks' van pulling into the parking lot.

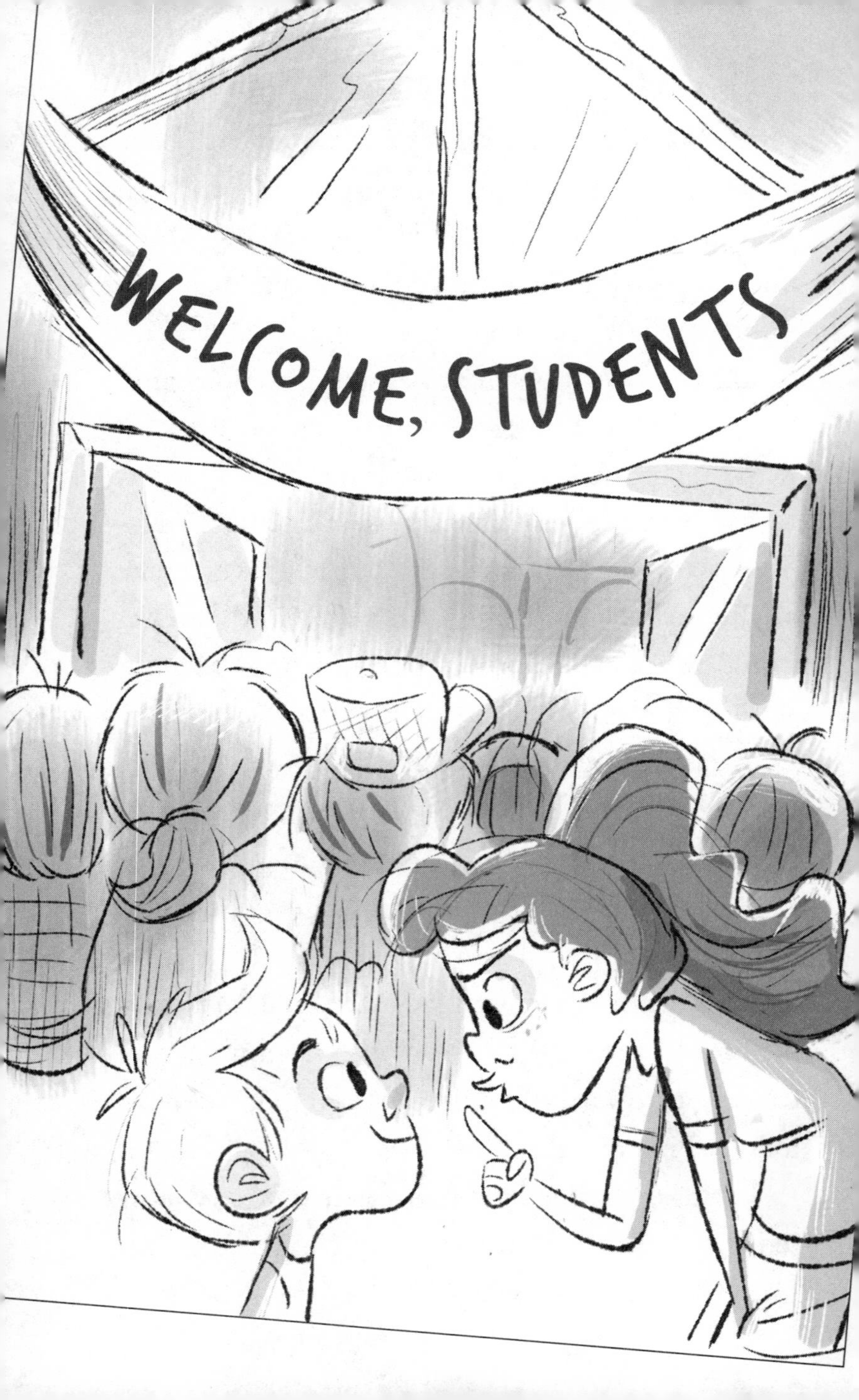
WELCOME, STUDENTS

"Gramps and Uncle Cork are here now," she whispered to Finn. "I'm going to tell them what happened, and they'll figure out how to get you back to school."

Footsteps and gasps muffled their conversation. For just inside the door of the museum, there were dozens of creepy masks and wax heads scattered around the room on pedestals. The class fanned out into the lobby, admiring all the gross stuff.

Finn replied, "I don't wanna go back to school. I want to stay with Christine."

Molly saw the disappointment in her brother's face. But it wasn't her fault. He had to learn his limits, and sneaking onto the fourth-grade field trip was simply not acceptable. She hated when she had to mother Finn, but when she was the only person who could see him causing trouble, it was impossible for her to shirk the responsibility.

As everyone else checked out all the cool stuff in the front lobby, Molly pulled her brother into a tucked-away coat closet. In the relative safety of the hiding space, she hurried to say, "You do *not* get to go with us. You get to go back to school, because your teacher is probably very worried about you.

Mom didn't call this morning to report you absent, so they're going to be expecting you. When Mrs. Risdall calls home to check on you, no one is going to be there to answer the phone. And then, when Mom gets home from work, she's going to panic when she hears a message from school saying you're not there. She'll be terrified."

Finn's big brown eyes settled on Molly's mouth. He couldn't look directly at her. She could see tears welling up in the corners of his eyes. "I didn't think about that."

"You should have," Molly said, more harshly than she'd meant to. If Grandpa's magic were more powerful, like it had been when he was younger, she could ask him to zip them back to the moment before the bus left from school. They could have a do-over, and this time, Molly would get her brother off the bus before they left school. But Grandpa Quill's Quirk was often unreliable when they had to leap back more than a few minutes, and Molly didn't want to do anything that might risk ruining their fun field-trip day. She sighed, and resigned herself to the fact that Finn was here. "Right now, I'm the only person who knows where you are.

An adult needs to know so that they can fix this. I'm going to tell Gramps and he can figure it out."

Just as she said that, Uncle Cork came barreling around the corner into the coat closet. He looked around, and Molly was pretty sure his eyes landed on Finn. Eyes narrowed, he asked, "What are you doing in here, Molly?"

Molly stared at him. "How did you know I was back here?"

"A hunch," he said. "So . . . ?"

Molly glanced at her brother, then looked back at her uncle. "Finn snuck on the bus. He's here now."

"I see." Cork reached into his pocket and pulled out a piece of gum. He handed it to Finn, who reluctantly stuffed it into his mouth and came into view.

Finn muttered, "I'm sorry. I didn't want to miss the field trip, and I didn't think anyone would really care that I'd tagged along once we were already here. No one will even notice me if I stay invisible."

"Ah," Cork said gently. "But they *will* notice you're missing back at school. Now, Molly, why

don't you go on ahead and join the rest of your
class. I'll deal with Mr. Finnegan, and see if we
can't sort this out somehow. You go on now, and
enjoy yourself."

Molly shuffled out of the coat closet grate-
fully. In the lobby, Christine was standing with a
man who had big ears, a loose-lipped smile,
and tiny little eyes. He was as friendly-looking
as Christine was intense. Molly hoped she
would be in the man's group. He seemed like
he would be much more fun. But then again,
Christine did seem to be a better match for a
Halloween museum—so maybe she'd be a bigger

help when it came time for them to work on their Spook Style challenge.

"Where have you been?" Pen asked, coming over to stand beside Molly.

Molly explained the situation with their brother.

Pen twisted at the curl behind her left ear. "What are we going to do?"

"Nothing," Molly said. "I handed him over to Cork. He's going to talk to Gramps and figure it out. We just need to enjoy ourselves, he said."

"Nice." Pen nodded. "Did you see some of these wax heads? They're crazy." She pulled Molly toward a giant ogre head that was encased in glass.

The girls walked around with their classmates for a few minutes, marveling over the real-looking creeps and monster heads that filled the lobby. There was a creature that looked like a werewolf whose mouth was wide open in a giant roar. A pale vampire made out of wax was partially melted. "That one is made of cake," a quiet voice murmured, right behind Molly.

Molly and Pen spun around, coming face-to-face with Christine. "Cake?" Pen asked.

"Cake. One of our employees works for a bakery most of the year, and she's begun to design some of her displays out of cake, cereal, and white chocolate."

"That is really cool," Pen said.

"And delicious," Christine agreed. She was slightly less creepy-looking up close, but Molly couldn't keep herself from stepping back a bit to get some distance. "We actually use a lot of food here at the museum. Many of the touch-and-feel displays are almost all food."

"Touch-and-feel?" Molly wondered.

Christine smiled mysteriously. "Sensory boxes. You'll see." She glanced at the clock. "I guess we'd better get started. I want to make sure you all have plenty of time for your own creations at the end of the day."

Christine floated away as Grandpa Quill and Uncle Cork strode purposefully over to the girls. Finn trailed along behind them, chomping his gum. "I talked to Mr. Intihar, then called the school and sorted everything out," Grandpa Quill said.

"Oh, good," said Molly.

"Partly good," Grandpa murmured. "They know where he is and Mr. Intihar isn't in trouble for any of this, so *that's* good. But unfortunately, neither Cork nor I can leave here to return him to school. We're the chaperones for your field trip, and museum rules require an adult to be with each group at all times."

Pen shook her head. "But . . . but, how will he get back to school? Can't Mr. Intihar just cover for one of you while you bring him back?"

"Nope," Cork said. "Your teacher doesn't count as one of the chaperones. And when we told Mr. Intihar that Finn was here, his solution was to have Finn stick around until your mum can come to retrieve him after her shift at the diner. He was mighty concerned about how Finn had gotten past him onto the bus—and he felt very guilty about it all—but I think we smoothed it over as best we could."

"But Mom's not done working for a couple hours!" Molly protested. "And she doesn't have a car."

Grandpa shrugged. "Martha offered to drive her over this afternoon—she's been meaning to check this place out, so she said she'd be happy to give them a lift."

"So this means Finn gets to stay?" Pen growled.

Finn smiled. "Yep."

"It's only for a few hours," Gramps said. "He owes Mr. Intihar a mighty big apology for this mess, and I imagine he will be in *big* trouble with your mother when she gets here. But that's neither here nor there—for the moment, he gets to stay. It's our only choice."

Molly and Pen both glared at their brother.

"Don' worry girls," said Cork with a wink. "I'm going to keep an extra eye on him—I'll keep the kid out of your way. Promise."

CHAPTER 10

Boxes of YUCK

"If the group with Mr. Mustache will follow me, we'll start our tour of the museum at the Wall of Smells." Christine gestured to Grandpa Quill's group.

Penelope looked over at Molly and rolled her eyes. *Of course* she'd gotten Christine as her guide, she thought. Now she had Christine *and* Nolan for the whole day. She twisted at the curl behind her ear again. This was just super. She took a deep breath and focused. Her nerves relaxed when Norah wrapped an arm through hers and said,

"Come on, Pen. Let's stick together. I get totally creeped by scary stuff, so I'm going to need someone to keep me from freaking out today."

Molly smiled. Calm, quiet Norah would be the perfect distraction for Pen's wandering imagination. Maybe if Pen had something other than her own magical mind to focus on, she could let herself relax a bit. Sometimes, Molly had realized, when Penelope was too worried about her magic acting up, it almost made things worse for her.

Mr. Intihar trailed along after Pen's group. He planned to float between the two halves of his class throughout the day, but was starting with Grandpa Quill's group. The girls wondered if their mom had warned him about Grandpa's tendency to doze off. She had a feeling their teacher would be keeping an extra eye on Gramps, just like Uncle Cork had promised to keep an extra eye on Finn.

After Penelope and her group followed Christine out of the front hall of the museum, Molly's team was left alone in the entryway. The other guide—who introduced himself as Tom—waved to Uncle Cork. "Hello there, Mad Hatter. I take it you're our chaperone for today?"

"Hello yourself," answered Cork. "And yessiree, I am your chaperone."

"Well, you're not *my* chaperone. Though sometimes I do need one," Tom said, his big ears wiggling. "I see you wore a costume of your own to the museum."

"You could say that," answered Uncle Cork with a wink. Today, he was wearing another of his elaborate outfits. His checkered pants were chopped off at the knee, and he had long striped socks pulled partway up his calves. He was wearing a bright yellow pair of loafers and, as usual, had topped off his look with the same snazzy cap. Now he took off the cap and waved it in Tom's direction. The rainbow sweatband pressed his crazy hair into place. "Even brought a spare headpiece, just in case I lose the first."

The other kids in Molly's group stared at her uncle. "That's *your* uncle?" Stella said, rather loudly.

"Yep," answered Molly. Though some people might have been embarrassed about Cork's strange style, she was proud that she got to have her uncle Cork as the chaperone for her group. He was eccentric and strange and a little bit embarrassing;

but he was also very confident, and fun, and . . . out there—in a good way. She admired him a lot.

Molly was so used to the rest of the members of her family, who were always trying to hide their oddities around others. Each one of them was stuffed full of personality and quirks, but none of the rest of the family seemed to embrace it the way Uncle Cork did. He wore his zaniness on his sleeve—literally (that day's sweater was blue-and-white-striped and had a big, fluffy cow embroidered onto the center, as well as smaller cows on each of the elbows).

Stella giggled. "He looks fun."

Molly smiled back. "He is."

Tom spoke quickly, telling the kids their schedule for the day. Then he asked each person in the group to write out a name tag. "I don't care what name you put on it—this is a museum about costumes and disguises and creating characters, so feel free to make up a new name if you want. I just need to know what you want me to call you."

Molly thought for a long moment, then finally settled on her real name for the name tag. As twins, she and Penelope were often mistaken for each other, so sometimes it felt good to just be herself without any of that confusion. Some of the other kids giggled as they wrote down their nicknames or famous movie-star names or the names of their pets. It seemed like many people were excited to have the chance to pretend to be someone else for the day. As a Quirk, Molly was tired of pretending to be someone she wasn't all the time—sometimes she wished everyone could just *know* she was part of a really zany, fabulous family full of quirks.

She glanced down at her brother, who had slipped a name tag off the table after everyone else was finished. He chewed the top of a marker thoughtfully, then scribbled "Poopsy" on the tag. This caused him to come down with a case of the giggles. Molly tried to ignore him.

After they all had name tags on, Tom led them out the other side of the front hall and into another large room. "Today, we're going to learn about how to make Halloween truly spooky as we wind our way through Spook City. Let's start with a bit of a quiz! Usually, we say that people have how many senses?"

"Five!" shouted Raade.

"Right," Tom said excitedly, pointing at him. "Five senses—that most people are aware of, anyway. And what are they?"

"Um, touch?" guessed Raade. Tom nodded.

"Hearing," piped up Molly.

"Smell," said Finn. Again, Molly glared at him. He wasn't supposed to participate.

Stella added, "Taste!"

Finally, Uncle Cork bellowed out, "Sight!"

"Right," said Tom. "Sight, smell, touch, hearing, and taste. So for something to really *get* us, it should activate all five of those senses. Right?"

The kids all nodded.

"So that's what we're going to do today—we're going to activate all five of your senses and see how much creepier things are when you punch them all into high gear." Tom raised his hands in the air and clapped. "So! In this room, we've set up a sensory buffet. Inside each of these boxes, you'll find something that *feels* really gross. It's going to really get your sense of *touch* buzzing."

Cork leaned down and whispered into Molly's ear, "I didn't know we were going to be learning on this field trip. Bonus!"

"I want everyone to take turns reaching into each of these sensory boxes and let your fingers explore the contents inside. You can't see or smell or hear or taste anything—how does that change your perception of what's in there?" Tom ushered the group to different stations and urged everyone to reach inside the covered boxes scattered around the room.

Molly reluctantly poked her hand into a large blue box. Inside, she discovered a bunch of slimy, round lumps. Tom sidled over and whispered, "Eyeballs." Molly snatched her hand back out of

the box and wiped the oozy stuff off on the cloth hanging from the edge of the box. The look on her face made Tom laugh.

Finn, who'd been mostly quiet and well behaved so far, shoved his hand into the box and yelped, "Yucko!"

The rest of the sensory boxes were filled with more gross, fascinating stuff: wiggly intestines, a wrinkled brain, gooey worms. Molly and Stella went around the room together, trying to figure out what the museum staff might have used to make each of the sensory boxes. She thought the intestines felt a little like cooked spaghetti.

"Olives," Finn whispered, creeping up behind Molly.

"What?" Molly searched the room for Uncle Cork, but he was nowhere to be seen. Several of the wooden sensory boxes were around the corner, behind a big display wall—he was probably back there with the rest of the class and Tom. Molly was irritated her uncle had left Finn on his own. She wasn't supposed to be keeping an eye on Finn, so she wanted Cork to get him out of her hair.

"The eyeballs. They're olives." Finn smiled. "Am I right, or am I left?"

"I don't know, Finn." Molly glanced at Stella, who shrugged.

"Let's take a quick peeksy-poo. I'll be able to tell you all the secrets they're keeping from us in no time." Finn slipped on the X-ray glasses that he had gotten as a gift from Uncle Cork. He squinted and leaned in closer to the eyeball box. Then he lifted the glasses off his nose and dropped them back into place again. Finally, he frowned. "*Pfffft.* These things must not work on wood."

Finn took the glasses off, examined them, then stuffed them in his back pocket. Before Molly or Stella realized what he was doing, Finn began to lift the top off the sensory box. At first it wouldn't budge, so he grabbed the edges of the wooden box in both hands and began to shake it. Inside, a bunch of somethings bonked around and around. Grunting from the effort of lifting the box, Finn said, "I know it's olives! I can smell 'em. Niblet would love to get his little hands on this box of yum—it's a box full of his favorite snack."

Suddenly, Uncle Cork zoomed around the corner, yelling, "Stop, Finnegan!"

Finn dropped the box back on the table and put his hands up. "I didn't do anything," he lied.

"The boxes are for touching, not peeking," Cork said, leading Finn away.

Molly smirked. "Good timing, Uncle Cork. You came around the corner at just the right moment!"

Cork nodded back at her. "My timing is always impeccable."

"In peck a bull?" asked Finn, crinkling his nose.

"Impeccable," Cork clarified. "That means perfect. My timing is spot-on." He winked at Molly.

It was clear Cork had meant it when he said he'd keep a close eye on Finn, because he continued to have impeccable timing throughout the rest of the morning. It seemed that every time Finn was about to create a problem or get into trouble, Uncle Cork would swoop in to pull him away just in the nick of time.

While their group was exploring Costume Alley— using their sense of sight—Tom captivated the group with all kinds of tricks of the costume trade. He showed them witches' fingernails and monster fur and told them how they used colored contacts to make actors' eyes look extra-creepy in haunted houses. Everyone was busy admiring a lush velvet vampire cape and gathering ideas for their own Spook Style designs, when Finn wandered off and went missing. Cork somehow managed to find him almost immediately, wrapped up inside a pile of zombie rags.

Then, when they walked through the Corridor of Sounds, Cork was the only one who realized Finn had ducked behind the thick curtain where they kept all the sound equipment.

Next, they stopped to sniff monstrously horrible scents—garlic, moldy shoe, rotten fish, "death" breath, dirty hair—at the Wall of Smells. Mr. Intihar caught up to their group then, and Finn waited until Uncle Cork was busy chatting with him to make his next move. As soon as Cork's attention was elsewhere, Finn slipped through an open door into a closet. But moments later, Cork pulled open the door and caught him red-handed, trying on spooky masks in the closet.

Molly was impressed. She had gotten used to being the only one who could see Finn when he was invisible and particularly mischievous. But it was like Cork had some sort of sixth sense that let him just *know* where Finn was going to be from minute to minute. "Oh!" Molly gasped when she considered that. They'd been talking about the senses all day, and she hadn't even considered . . . What if Cork's Quirk was some sort of sixth sense?

She decided to ask. But Cork didn't answer.

"Is that it?" Molly pressed as they moved to the next room. She lowered her voice to a whisper. "Is that your Quirk?"

Cork's eyes twinkled. He lifted his hat slightly to scratch behind his ear. Finally, he said, "Nope. I've got the same five senses as you do. Some of mine might just be a bit more refined than some of yours." He waggled his eyebrows—then walked away.

CHAPTER 11

Hall of Freaks

When they met up with the other group for lunch, Molly told Penelope what Cork had said. "What does *that* mean?" Pen asked. "His senses are 'more refined'?"

"I have no idea." Molly shrugged. "I just know that he's really good at keeping an eye on Finn. I'm so used to being the one who always catches him making mischief. It's really cool that Uncle Cork is helping to keep him out of trouble today. I honestly thought it would be awful having our brother here, but with Uncle

Cork around, I'm not really noticing Finn much at all."

"I've been able to avoid Nolan most of the day, too," said Pen. "Norah and I spent most of the morning chatting so we wouldn't get freaked out by the costumes and props. So far, so good."

The girls joined some of their other classmates to eat, and the groups compared notes from the morning. Everyone was excited to visit the Hall of Freaks after lunch, since both Tom and Christine had been talking it up all day. None of them knew what it was, but it sounded awesome.

Penelope, who sometimes got a nervous stomach, hadn't sniffed any of the scents at the Wall of Smells. When Molly and their other friends told her what she'd missed, Penelope lost her appetite for lunch. After a lot of discussion, no one was any more certain about what any of the yucky things were inside the sensory boxes, but everyone agreed that they didn't want to think about it while they were eating.

While the group was still chatting and eating, Tom and Christine called for attention. "Now that you've all had a chance to be inspired by the Spook

Style in our museum," Tom said, "it's time for our two groups to split up again and get to work on the Spook Style challenge."

The students from room six cheered. Finn cheered along with everyone else. He attracted a lot of attention when he *moo*ed, and the girls both wondered how much longer he was going to be hanging around. Bree's shift ended at lunch, so she should be there soon.

Penelope wondered if, when Molly told their

mom about how great their uncle had been with Finn all morning, she might start to warm up to Cork a little more. She would, at least, have to thank him for everything he'd done to help with the situation—and maybe, Pen thought, their mom would finally figure out how to relax around Uncle Cork. Then the conversation about the day would get them talking. If they talked, then soon they'd be laughing together, and before long they'd realize how much they enjoyed hanging out.

Christine floated around the room, speaking so quietly that everyone had to be totally silent to hear her. "As your teacher may have told you, we want to see what kinds of creeps your minds can devise. Hopefully you've picked up a lot of ideas for how to make something truly scary during your visit to the museum today. We've tickled your five senses with the treats of Halloween, and now we'd like to see what kinds of creations your teams can come up with to spook *us*."

"Oh, I'll spook you, that's for sure," boasted Nolan. "I have some seriously freaky ideas up my sleeve."

Tom beamed down at Nolan and said, "Excellent. I look forward to seeing what your group comes up with." He pranced around the room, his lips and ears bouncing with each step. "Each group will receive one plain mannequin to use as your base, and an identical closet of supplies. Christine and I will stay with the groups we worked with this morning, and we'll be your professional resources. If you need help figuring out makeup techniques, or if you need any kind of assistance with costumes, you can ask us to guide you. We will not, however, be giving you any kind of direction unless you ask a specific question."

Christine arched her eyebrow and gazed around at the groups. "Does that make sense to everyone? Do you have any questions?"

"When do we start?" blurted Nolan.

"Yeah!" shouted Finn. "I hafta leave soon, so let's get this show on the road."

Mr. Intihar gestured for Nolan to take the seat beside him, and Cork did the same with Finn.

Tom looked around, then said, "No more questions? Does anyone want to know what your team wins if we like your Spook Style creation best?"

"There's a winner?" asked Stella. "I thought it was just for fun."

Tom nodded. "It *is* about fun. But we also have a neat prize for the winning team. The Spook City Haunted House is open on Halloween only. All of you on the winning team will get free passes to visit our spook show with your families before you go trick-or-treating tomorrow evening." There was a lot of cheering. Even Pen got excited before she remembered that she probably wouldn't be going to the haunted house—unless she knew ahead of time what was hiding behind all the corners, her imagination would run wild.

After a moment, Tom shushed them again. "Not only will you get to bring your families to the haunted house, but you will actually get to have a hand in scaring them. Each member of the winning team will get to join us as guest spooks for an hour, dressed in your Halloween finest. You will be a *part* of the haunted house."

"What?!" screeched Nolan. "Not really?"

"Really," said Tom. "And I can assure you that being behind the scenes in a haunted house is even more fun than visiting one as a guest.

You'll be given help with makeup to spice up your costumes if you need it, and we'll loan you accessories if you'd like. As a member of the Spook City haunt team, you'll have the opportunity to really freak out your families. How does that sound?"

The class erupted with excitement. "Calm down, everyone," said Mr. Intihar. But it was no use—everyone was bubbling with ideas for their team challenge, and now *everyone* wanted to win.

Somehow, Christine's soft, gentle voice floated up and over the group and drew their attention back to the front of the room. "If you've all finished with lunch, you can follow us into the Hall of Freaks. There, you'll be able to gather some final inspiration before we break out into our teams to begin the competition." She looked over her shoulder as she moved out of the front hall. "Please. Follow me."

The class stood up and hustled after her. At the end of a long hallway, Christine passed under a tall archway. On the other side of the arch, the kids all looked around in amazement. Norah reached for Penelope's hand, closed her eyes tight, and Pen guided her friend into the enormous room.

The Hall of Freaks truly was a hall of freaks. Enormous monsters surrounded them and made the girls feel like they were in a horror film come to life. Though the creatures were created out of mannequins and masks and makeup and costumes, they looked frightfully real.

The fourth graders all fanned out across the room, keeping a safe distance from the creatures that gazed menacingly down at them. Soft, spooky music was piping into the room from somewhere. The hall was ripe with the smell of rotten leaves and something distinctly *dead*—Molly noticed that the odor was so strong she could almost taste it. It felt like a gentle wind was kissing the back of Penelope's neck, making it seem like something was creeping up behind her. Their senses were immediately activated, and the whole experience was beyond creepy.

"Whoa," muttered Joey.

"I don't feel well," said Izzy, looking as if she were close to tears. She and Norah huddled together in a corner, trying to keep their eyes averted from the creatures that surrounded them on all sides.

Molly felt a shiver run through her body as she locked eyes with a still-as-a-statue wolf-man. She quickly backed away and scooted several feet to the side—but still, she could have sworn the creature's eyes followed her as she moved. Penelope, whose face had gone white as a sheet, reached for her sister's hand. "I don't like this place."

"You're okay," Molly promised. "It's all fake. Think of all the great Halloween costume ideas you can get in here. Forget Cinderella—this stuff is fierce."

"I know," Pen whispered back. She slammed her eyes closed. "But I'm worried about them coming to life."

"Don't make that happen," warned Molly, pulling Pen away from the rest of the group.

"I'm trying not to," Pen said. "But that wind on my neck . . . it's making it really hard for me to concentrate on anything other than what might happen if this whole room turned real."

Molly looked into her sister's eyes. "You've got this. Ignore the smell, and that awful taste in your mouth, and pretend the wind isn't there. Pretend you're back in room six, getting ready for group work. Think about how much Norah needs you to be strong right now. Imagine you're in a cone of safety."

Cork, who had Finn firmly by the hand, came over just as Molly was finishing her pep talk. Their uncle said, "But don't push your Quirk down too far, Penelope. You've got something special inside of you, and you can really use it in situations like this. That imagination of yours is something else— let it give you an advantage in the challenge."

Pen stared at him. "But what if my Quirk gets out of control and then something terrible happens? No one can know about us," she said desperately.

"Would it really be so terrible if people found out about your magic?" Cork asked in a hushed voice. He looked from Molly to Penelope seriously. "What's the worst that could happen?"

"We'd have to move," Molly said simply. "It's already happened twenty-six times. We love Normal. We want to stay here."

Cork shrugged. "So stay."

"We *can't* stay if people find out about our Quirks!" Molly said, a bit more loudly than she'd intended to. She felt like she and her family had

had this conversation at least a hundred times. They all knew exactly what would happen if someone found out about them—they would move. That's just the way it was, the way it had always been. Texas, Indiana, Hawaii? Who knew what their next stop would be.

"Why can't you stay?" pressed Cork. Grandpa Quill, who had been wandering around the room staring into each monster's face, sauntered over and stood with the rest of his family.

"Why not?" Pen stared at Cork, openmouthed. "Because no one can know about us. Mom says. That's just the way it is. If anyone finds out about our Quirks, terrible things will happen." She nodded, but Molly noticed her sister didn't look entirely convinced.

Cork sighed. "That's the way it is, eh?" He was suddenly angry. Little droplets of spit came from his mouth when he hissed, "*What* terrible things? How do you know?"

Molly had a million reasons for why no one could know about them, but something about Cork's expression made Molly pause. "Does anyone know about your Quirk, Uncle Cork?"

Cork glanced at Grandpa Quill, who gave the slightest shake of his head.

"No," Cork said, obviously lying.

"You've told someone?" Pen said, incredulous. "*We* don't even know what your Quirk is, and yet someone *else* knows? Someone outside the family?"

Cork nodded and began to say something else. But suddenly, they shot back in time.

Obviously, Grandpa Quill didn't want Cork talking about it. The trouble was, Gramps couldn't rewind Molly's memory—she was immune to his magic. Everyone else would snap back in time and have no memory of what had just happened and what they'd talked about. Molly could feel time flipping backward, but that was about it. He couldn't make her forget what she'd already heard.

Grandpa zipped them back about a minute, and once again Cork was saying, "That imagination of yours is something else—let it give you an advantage in the challenge." Suddenly, Grandpa Quill dashed across the room. He was moving faster than Molly had ever seen him move before. His jiggly stomach flopped up and down as he ran toward Molly, Pen, Cork, and Finn.

Before Molly could take the conversation in the same direction it had been going in just moments before Grandpa Quill had hit his rewind button, Gramps burst in, "Yes! Let your special imagination give you an advantage, my dear. But not *too* much of an advantage, as we certainly don't need anything crazy to happen. Now, shouldn't we join the rest of our group and start our monstrous creation?"

Penelope looked from Grandpa, to Cork, to Molly. "Um, okay?"

"Okay," Grandpa Quill said. "Now is not the time or place to continue this discussion." He looked back at Molly as he led her twin away and across the room.

Molly was determined to pick this thread of conversation back up as soon as she could. Without Grandpa Quill around, she hoped she'd have a chance to ask Cork plenty more questions as the afternoon went on.

CHAPTER 12

Creep Closets

After the class took a few minutes to explore the frightening Hall of Freaks, Tom and Christine showed each of the teams to their Spook Style closet. As promised, each of the groups was given a plain brown mannequin—the kind you might find in mall store windows—and shelves and shelves full of costumes, makeup, wigs, fur, fake skin in all sorts of colors, and a whole wall of accessories. There were also several boxes in each closet that were labeled clearly enough to make their contents obvious: SOUND CHIPS, SMELL PACKETS, FAKE BLOOD, INSECTS, TEETH.

"We use a lot of things just like these in our haunted house, so you guys get to work with professional-grade stuff here," explained Tom. The groups both took a few minutes to explore their closets, pulling things off the shelves when they found something that looked cool. "Christine and I can help you with makeup, if you need it. But please: try to create your characters on your own. You'll really bring your monsters to life if the inspiration comes straight from your imaginations into the world. It will also give you some great practice for building your own Halloween costumes tomorrow night."

"Okay, everybody, I know what we're doing for our monster," Nolan announced to his group as soon as Tom stopped talking. He was speaking so loudly that the other half of the class could hear him plainly, too. "I drew up some designs this week. I've got our winner. Let me show you."

Nolan pulled out his drawings of silly monsters and hairy, long-clawed beasts. Nearby, Norah whispered to Penelope, "I drew a bunch of ideas for Halloween creeps, too." She hung her head sadly. "I had a feeling I wouldn't even get to show anyone."

Pen watched with disgust as Nolan tried to take over and boss the rest of the group around. She was sick and tired of Nolan having so much control over her and everyone else. He was always bragging and trying to run all the recess games on the playground, and now he was trying to take over their monster design, too? Nuh-uh.

Not this time, Penelope thought to herself. Norah had ideas, and she was sure other people in their group did, too. It wasn't fair to the rest of them that Nolan was trying to take advantage of everyone else with his loud personality.

Without another thought, she quipped, "You're not in charge, Paulson." Nolan spun around and frowned at her.

Norah, Amelia, Joey, and the rest of their group stood between Pen and Nolan. Everyone watched eagerly as they faced off. Grandpa Quill twirled the edges of his mustache, whistling with pride— Pen had crept out of the shadows and was taking charge!

Since she had created her own pet monster, Pen was fairly confident that she *knew* monsters. But it wasn't just herself she was fighting for—she knew every one of her teammates had a super imagination hidden inside their bodies, and they all had every right to be a part of their group design.

Nolan began pulling things off the shelves in the closet, tossing them into the air. He was acting like he hadn't heard Penelope. He tossed a thick clump of dark fur on the ground then dumped a pair of hairy black gloves on top of it.

Pen put her hands on her hips, stepped forward, and said, loudly, "Stop it! We're doing this as a team. Everyone gets a say in our creation." Nolan just stared at her, his eyebrows pulled together. Pen continued, "It's like the five senses we've been learning about today. If we all work together and combine our ideas, instead of letting you make all the decisions, our Spook Style creation is going to be a whole lot spookier."

Nolan stopped pawing through the closet. Pen waited for him to say something, all the while listening to her heart thudding in her chest. She'd never stood up to anyone like that before—other than her brother and sister, of course. She felt a bit queasy as she waited to hear what Nolan would say. She tried to step backward, to disappear among the

friends who were standing behind her. She wanted nothing more than to run and hide, but her feet were frozen in place. Her body was holding her there, forcing her to stay strong.

Finally, Nolan shrugged and said, "Okay."

Penelope's breath rushed out of her in a loud whoosh. "Great." Norah smiled at Penelope, and Pen felt as good as she would have if she'd just gotten a perfect score on a math test.

Christine glided over to the group as everyone began throwing their ideas into the brainstorming pot. When it came to creating their

Spook Style, some people had monsters on the mind, others were thinking of witches, and Joey had the idea to create something that looked like a zombified vampire. After a lot of discussion, they soon had an idea of how to create a creature with an ogre-like head on a slender, rotting witch's body. "Sounds like we're on a roll over here," Christine said. "I can't wait to see what it looks like when you're finished." Pen's group got to work, knowing they had to work quickly since they'd lost some of their design time to arguing.

Meanwhile, Molly's group had already begun to accessorize their creature. They'd made a large, hairy beast that looked like a chubby Bigfoot with one big, weepy eye and a body filled with olive-green spots. The group giggled as more and more items were added to their creation. Soon the creature looked like a potluck table at the end of a party—here a little of this, there a little of that, and everywhere a whole lot of mess.

Izzy and Molly were busy trying to turn their spook's hands into gnarled, bloody stumps. They had found some fake skin that they had wrapped around the mannequin's

arms to make it look like its hands had been chopped off in some sort of violent battle. Now they were dousing the hands in fake blood that was dripping all over the floor.

Tom saw what was happening and assured them, "It's no big deal. We expect messes around here. When we're in the midst of creating, things need to get torn apart before we can create something wonderful. Invent away—we'll take care of cleanup later!"

Finn, who was sitting miserably to the side, cheered up when Tom gave him a box of props and a small doll to use for designing his own spook. Finn was delighted to be included, especially when he knew he deserved nothing more than a time-out after what he'd done.

Mr. Intihar walked between the two groups with Uncle Cork and Grandpa Quill. The three men chatted about Scotland, and their favorite candies, and also about Bree. Molly tried to listen in to their conversation, hoping she'd learn more about why her mother was so nervous around their uncle, but could only hear out-of-place snippets of their conversation.

Just as the monsters were nearing completion, Molly spotted her mom crossing through the Hall of Freaks. Beside her, Martha Chalupsky—the owner of Crazy Ed's—was ogling all the creatures that filled the space. Bree, however, only had eyes for Finn. She looked absolutely furious as she stormed across the room.

"Time to go, Finnegan," Bree announced. Finn tried to slither out of view, but even he knew it was no use trying to be sneaky anymore. He was already in trouble, and any further mischief would just make his life worse. He knew that if his mom got *really* mad at him, she might even make tofu for dinner.

See, the easiest way to punish Finn was with food. Finn was such a picky eater that if Bree really wanted to teach him a lesson, she'd make all his most-hated foods for a week. It was a sure-fire punishment.

"Young man, we are out of here," announced Bree. "We will discuss your punishment at home. Right now, I need you to stand up, thank your hosts, and follow me directly to the door."

Finn did as he was told. He stuffed the doll and the tiny costumes back into a box, thanked Tom, and shuffled over to his mother's side. "Thanks for hanging out with me all day, Uncle Cork."

Uncle Cork smiled and tipped his hat at Finn. "'Twas my pleasure, young man. Though I hope next time we get a day to spend together, it will be under better circumstances. I know how fun it can be to play around with your Quirk, but believe me when I tell you it's best not to use your unique powers for making mischief."

Bree shot Cork a grateful look. "Thank you for keeping an eye on him today. I'm terribly sorry for the inconvenience."

"Happy to do it," Cork said. At this point, both Molly and Penelope had turned their attention away from their teams' monster building and were watching their mom and uncle with great interest. Bree stepped forward and gave her brother a small hug. The girls grinned at each other—this was major progress!

Bree waved to the girls and turned to leave. But before she could step through the grand archway leading out of the Hall of Freaks, she heard a shrill scream. The Quirks, Martha, Tom, Christine, and all of room six turned their attention to the source of the scream: Norah.

Norah had turned pasty white and was frozen in place with her arm pointing at something inside the closet. Nolan, Amelia, and Joey all backed away from the closet en masse, their faces filled with fear. The minute Molly looked at her twin sister, she knew exactly what had happened. Something in Penelope's creep closet had come to life. Clearly, their Spook Style team challenge was about to get a *lot* more interesting.

125

CHAPTER 13

It's . . . Alive?

"**Oh no,** oh no, oh no . . . ," Penelope muttered, covering her eyes with her hands.

Molly ran to her sister and shushed her. "It's okay." She looked up, and for the first time got a good look at the *thing* that had come to life inside Pen's team's closet. She sucked in a breath and tried not to freak out.

A hairy hand was creeping forward out of the closet. It looked like a five-legged spider, but had three eyes and a mouth on its back. A double row of knifelike shark teeth gnashed and clacked as the hand zagged forward toward the fourth graders. Slimy yellow drool oozed out of its mouth and drizzled across its back and down onto the floor.

Wisely, Uncle Cork jumped forward and slammed the door to the closet closed. The hand was trapped inside the creep closet. But a moment later, a sound like a wood chipper buzzed inside the closet, and both girls were pretty sure the hand was trying to chew its way out.

When Norah burst into panicked tears, Grandpa Quill leaped into action. He stood up, stretched, and seconds later Molly could feel herself getting tugged backward through time. *Zip!* It felt like she'd been ripped off her feet and tossed backward. No matter how much Grandpa Quill rewound, Molly always thought it felt weird to get tossed through time.

When the whole group landed two minutes back with a lurch and a bump, Bree was once again giving Cork a hug and thanking him for his help. Grandpa Quill slouched in the corner of the room, dozing merrily. Time-twisting always made him drowsy.

Molly rushed over to her sister. "Pen, we've got a problem." She quietly and quickly explained what had happened before their grandpa rewound time. Penelope's eyes widened as she went into panic mode. "Don't freak out. That's just going to make it worse," Molly reminded her.

"I turned a prop alive!" Pen whispered urgently. "A walking, chomping, hairy hand! What could *be* worse?"

Molly cringed. "Well, it could have been the whole monster that came to life." As soon as she said it, she realized she ought not have said anything at all.

Penelope whipped around, checking out the progress on her group's Spook Style creation. Nolan was standing beside the monster, pretending to make it talk. Norah and Amelia were putting long, moldy-looking fingernails on the creature's bony hands. Several other kids were testing out the sound chips, and Christine was holding two pieces of clay that looked like rotten ears.

As Molly watched, one of the bony hands squeezed closed around Amelia's wrist. Amelia ripped her arm away and stared at their creation. "Cut it out, Nolan," she scolded, giving their classmate a dirty look.

"I didn't do anything," Nolan snapped back.

"You made it touch me," said Amelia. "It's creepy."

"Did not," argued Nolan.

Again, the witchy ogre flexed its fingers.

"There!" said Amelia, pointing. "You made it move. Stop that."

Christine, who'd been watching the group intently, stared at their creation with great interest.

She tilted her head to the side and focused on the spook's hand. Once again, it flexed a finger—next, it bent its arm into the slightest curve.

Penelope closed her eyes and hummed. Anything to try to drag her mind away from the images that were floating around inside her skull. Anything to make her imagination *not* think about what could happen if their creatures came to life.

"Wait!" Uncle Cork called out just as Bree dragged Finn through the archway toward home. He was watching Penelope and Molly closely. "Bree, come back here. We need you for a wee moment."

Molly held Penelope's shoulders still, trying to convey a sense of calm. She glanced over at Christine, who was now staring into her own hand. One of the gross ears was wiggling around in her palm, just the slightest bit. Molly knew what was happening: little by little, the creature was coming to life.

Behind her, Molly heard Cork asking Bree to clear the room. "Get Mr. Intihar to take the class out of here. Find some reason for him to evacuate. We've got a problem brewing."

Bree looked at Penelope, then at Molly, and finally at Pen's team's spook. It blinked at her, and Bree jumped into high gear.

"George." Bree sidled over to Mr. Intihar and spoke to him in her sweetest voice. "Don't you think it's about time for the class to take a break? Perhaps a snack outside in the fresh air would be a nice idea? Or maybe you can explore the rest of the museum again?"

"Uh." Mr. Intihar gave Bree a strange look. She focused her eyes on his, and his expression softened. "Sure! Yes, I think that's a great idea. Class! Let's take a break from our creations and revisit the other rooms in the museum. See if we can't get even more inspired."

"No way," blurted Nolan. "We're on a roll in here. We can't afford a break, Mr. I."

"You *will* take them out of here," Bree ordered. Just then, Pen's team's spook took a small step forward.

Nolan gasped. "It *did* move. What—?"

A few paces away, Cork shoved Molly's team's monster into the closet and slammed the door closed. The other students looked baffled. Stella asked, "Why did you just toss our spook in the closet?"

Cork gaped at the closed closet door and muttered, "Oh, golly . . . we've got a *monstrously* big problem!"

CHAPTER 14

MORE Underwear Monsters!

Molly held her sister close. Penelope took long, slow, deep breaths, but she was having a hard time calming herself. All day, she'd been squishing and poking at her magic, trying to keep it covered up so no one would find out about the secrets she was hiding. But like Cinderella at midnight, there was only so long she could pretend to be someone else, someone whose mind didn't go wild at the slightest suggestions. Penelope's disguise was fading—fast.

"Now! You need to go now," Bree told Mr. Intihar after seeing the frightened expression on Uncle

Cork's face. Molly knew how much her mom hated to use her magic on people—especially the people she cared about most—and silently thanked her for stepping in. "Please, George, leave the girls with me. I'll keep an eye on them."

Mr. Intihar barked at the class. "Room six, we are leaving right this minute, and that's final. Molly, Penelope, you're free to stay with your mother." The class, who weren't used to their teacher raising his voice, snapped into action. They lined up behind him, looking mournfully back at the piles of props and costumes and accessories littering the floor of the Hall of Freaks.

Norah looked curiously at Penelope. "Are you okay?" she asked.

Pen managed a weak smile for her friend. "I'm okay. Just going to help my mom get my brother out of here, then I'll come find you, okay?" Norah looked convinced, and Pen relaxed.

The ogre-witch twitched again. Cork dashed toward it and tossed it into the other closet.

"You'll have plenty of time to work on your monsters after a little break," Bree assured the fourth graders.

Several of the students in class gave her a strange look. "Where'd you come from, Mrs. Quirk?" asked Stella.

Bree smiled faintly. Her energy was fading. "I'm here to pick up Finn, of course. How lovely to see you again, Stella, dear."

Mr. Intihar led the class under the archway, out of the Hall of Freaks, and toward the front entrance hall. Tom, Christine, and Martha all looked on curiously. Bree turned to Martha. "Martha, maybe you should check out the rest of the museum with Mr. Intihar? He's supposed to have adult chaperones with the group, and my dad seems to be rather sleepy at the moment."

135

"Oh, sure," said Martha, oblivious to what was going on around her. "I'd love the chance to look around. Come find me whenever you're ready to head out, Bree."

Bree nodded, then turned her attention to Tom and Christine. They were shifting their focus from Penelope and Molly, to Cork and the closet, to Bree. "They left," Tom muttered. "Why did they *leave*?"

With a deep sigh, Bree said, "Your turn."

"Excuse me?" trilled Christine. "Who *are* you?" She looked at the wiggling ear in her hand once again. "What's up with this *ear*, Tom?"

"I'm a concerned parent," Bree muttered. "And I'm telling you, it's your turn to leave this room. We have some business to attend to. Leave the ogre ear, and go."

"You're not allowed to be in here alone," Christine said, shaking her purple-haired head. "The prop closets, and the statuaries, and all of our displays—"

"I'm afraid today we're going to be breaking a few rules," Bree replied. "Leave this room immediately, and don't ask any questions when you return."

While Bree worked her magic on Tom and Christine, Molly continued to comfort her sister. She'd almost forgotten Finn was still there, and startled when he came over and tapped Penelope on the shoulder. "Make mine come alive, too," he whispered.

Molly whipped around to look at her brother. "Stop it. You just want something to create a distraction so Mom will forget about your punishment!"

Finn shrugged.

Tom and Christine wandered out of the Hall of Freaks, looking completely bewildered. Bree's magic often had a strangely calming effect on people, leaving them in a sort of confused haze. But after Bree used her power of persuasion on too many people at a time, she was always twisted and dizzy and out of sorts. Now she spun in a few lazy circles, then collapsed on the floor. Cork rushed over and held out a piece of candy, which she happily took from him. A bit of sugar helped to restore her energy—at least a little bit.

"All righty," said Cork, taking control of the situation. With Grandpa Quill asleep in the corner, Bree twisted and weary, and Molly occupied with Penelope, he was the only person left to take charge. *Finn* certainly wasn't going to be much help. "Dad's done for the day, Bree's wiped, and we've got ourselves a bit of a situation." He reached for Molly's team's closed closet door, but stopped before he turned the handle. Cork looked at Penelope, then said, "I've got an idea for you."

Penelope glanced up miserably. "What?"

He peeked at the closed closet doors again and grimaced. Under his breath, Cork muttered, "That is one angry beast Molly's team made." In a louder voice, he said—calmly—to Pen, "Since it's clear that your imagination is running a wee bit wild at the moment, how about we try something different? Have you ever heard people suggest that if you get nervous in front of a room full of people, you could try picturing everyone in their underwear? That it might help make you less anxious?"

Pen nodded, then looked at her uncle. "Are you saying you want me to picture the monsters in their underwear?" A tiny smile slipped onto her face.

"Something like that," agreed Cork.

"An underwear monster!" Finn shrieked. "Just like my Halloween costume idea! 'Member when I was an underwear monster?"

Upon hearing her brother's outburst, Penelope groaned. At the suggestion, Pen's mind went wild again. Finn began to grow fur and tentacles. As he morphed into a sticky, underwear-clad beast, Finn yipped with glee. "Maybe I'll win the contest and I'll get to be in the haunted house!" he said merrily. "I'm going to win the Spook Style challenge! Me! *Meeeee!*"

Pen took another deep breath, and tried to control her thoughts. But as her monster-brother rolled around the floor, she found it impossible to erase the images in her mind. Halloween had always been difficult for Penelope, and her imagination had always been a little obsessed with monsters.

Suddenly, Cork jumped away from the prop closet doors. A moment later, something pounded from inside one of them. There was a scratchy sound from behind the other door. The Quirks all turned and stared.

"Okay," said Molly in a panic. "Picturing them in their underwear isn't working. How 'bout you think about how cute the class spooks might be when they're asleep? Or in silly costumes?" Cork yelped and stared at the closed doors again. Molly rushed on. "Anything, Penelope! Imagine anything

other than monsters. Breakfast, cupcakes, furry kittens—anything!"

But it was no use. Pen's mind was a whirling, swirling collection of monster images—and they were all bursting with life. She had been holding her imagination in, fretting about it leaking out of the cracks in her mind all day. Now there was no holding it back. Like a dam that could no longer keep rushing water at bay, Penelope's mind could no longer be contained.

Pen tried to picture her team's spook in a tutu, like the one Niblet sometimes wore to be cute. Then she tried to picture Molly's furry team monster wearing a funny hat. She squinted, rapidly redrawing the images in her mind. Just as the ideas for new monsters began to take shape in the farthest reaches of her imagination—

Thud!

There was another loud noise from inside the closet. Pen was startled and the silly pictures of monsters doing cute things disappeared in a *poof!* Both closet doors burst open, and the fourth grade's Spook Style critters came charging out into the Hall of Freaks.

CHAPTER 15

Monster Mash

Molly screamed as the creations came charging out of the closets. Beside her, Penelope flinched. As living, breathing monsters, the creatures were absolutely grotesque. When the kids had been working with their teams to design and create them, the monsters had seemed sort of funny. Silly, even. There was nothing that was actually real about them—just a lot of fun props and costumes that, altogether, made up cool-looking creeps.

But now, when they were alive and drooling and staring hungrily at the Quirk family, they were totally terrifying. The bloody stump arm Molly and Stella had put on their creature was oozing with fake blood. The creep's single, greasy eye blinked at the twins, then turned its focus to Cork and Bree across the room. In the corner, Grandpa Quill dozed, oblivious to the scene unfolding around them.

The ogre with a witch's body was unsteady on its feet. Its huge head lolled atop its skinny body, and it looked like it might keel over at any minute. Still, the creature was terrifying, and Molly didn't like the way it kept staring at them, as though it wanted something. Its fingers were long and gnarled, and the fingernails were grotesque.

Finn—eager to keep himself out of the monsters' line of sight—popped the gum out of his mouth and stuck it behind his ear. He went invisible. Though a moment earlier he'd been part boy, part monster (and had looked like he could be the other creatures' crazy-looking kid), he was now just a frightened-looking five-year-old again. All of Penelope's imagination was now focused on giving life to the room six spooks.

The monsters lurched forward.

The Quirks all crept back.

This little dance went on and on as the monsters edged ever closer to the family and the Quirks scooted away. Bree put her arms around her children and tried to comfort them. Still, Penelope shook with fear. Though she wanted to close her eyes to try to turn off the images in her mind, she simply couldn't. The creeps kept her unwavering attention, and Penelope knew it was going to be nearly impossible for her to calm herself enough to make the beasts turn into plain mannequins again.

When the initial surprise subsided, Molly took a deep breath and said, "We have to stay calm. Remember, these monsters are not *actually* alive. They're just alive because Pen imagined them that way."

From behind the wolf-man statue, Finn whispered, "Yeah, but Niblet wasn't real until Penelope made him that way . . . and he's *still* very alive."

Molly gulped. Finn was right. Niblet had been the only thing Pen's imagination had cooked up that hadn't gone away in a matter of a few minutes. Maybe there was some sort of loophole in her magic that made monsters want to stick around? She decided she'd rather not think about that as an option. "We need to figure out how to keep the monsters calm so Pen can relax again."

"They look hungry," Penelope said. She squinted, trying to take Cork's advice to picture them in silly costumes. She imagined the ogre in a bonnet, and the one-eyed beast in a flowery veil. But it wasn't working. They just looked creepier, and not at all funny.

"I hope they don't eat people," whined Finn.

Both monsters turned in the direction of Finn's voice and sniffed at the air. But then the two creeps noticed each other standing on either side of the Quirks. They turned and stared at each other—it was a monster face-off, and the Quirks were right in the middle of it.

"Uh-oh," said Uncle Cork, looking toward the archway and cocking his head just slightly. "The class is on their way back here. They'll get to the Hall of Freaks in less than a minute."

"What?" screeched Molly. "How do you know?"

"I jus' do," said Cork, warily watching the monsters out of his peripheral vision. After a quick look at Bree, he turned to Finn. "Hey, kid, give me your X-ray goggles, will ya?"

Finn shook his head. "Nope. They're busted."

"Give me the glasses. I can keep an eye on the class with them, and make sure I keep them away from here."

"I told you," said Finn, irritated. "The glasses don't work. I tried using them on the sensory boxes and they were junk."

"They work for me," blurted Cork. "If I put them on, I'll be able to see through walls and tell you where they are."

"If the glasses do work for you," said Molly, "please, could you keep an eye on the class and let us know if they get close? Then we can figure out some sort of distraction until we get this mess figured out."

Cork nodded. "That I can do." He squinted at the wall, then said, "Finn, young friend? We need someone to go out there and create a distraction right now. The class is gathered near the sensory boxes. I don't want to *tell* you to make mischief, but . . . could you go out there and do something to distract them?"

Finn ran out of the Hall of Freaks, eager to have such an important job—and the opportunity to escape the monster mash.

Molly took a deep breath and considered their options. The spooks were now growling at each other. The most important thing, she knew, was that no one else find out what was going on inside the Hall of Freaks. They had to keep the other students safe until the situation was under control.

"They really do look hungry," Penelope said again, tilting her head to the side.

A beat later, the furry creature roared and lunged at the ogre. The ogre reared back, and Bree, Molly, and Penelope screamed as little drops of spittle plopped out of the furry monster's mouth. Its breath smelled like beets and vinegar and made Molly feel sick.

The creatures charged at each other, starting up their own Spook Style competition. It was monster versus monster, and it seemed as though there was absolutely nothing any of the Quirks could do to stop the creepy war being waged inside the Hall of Freaks.

Suddenly, Molly had an idea. She ran across the room toward one of the prop closets. The monsters whipped around, watching her with great interest. For the moment, they were both much more interested in Molly than they were in each other.

"What are you doing?" Pen shouted. "We need to stick together."

Molly dug through the box labeled SMELL PACKETS. She grabbed one that said ROTTEN MEAT and popped it open. Then she tossed it across the Hall of Freaks and waited. Both creatures sniffed at the air.

They both lumbered toward the smell packet to investigate. The ogre's head lolled back and forth on its skinny body, making it move more slowly than the other monster. The furry beast reached the smell packet first, but when it reached out to grab it, the beast found that the bloody stumps Molly and Stella had put on the ends of its hands were of no use in picking things up.

Molly grabbed another smell packet, then another. Rapidly, she lobbed them across the room. The monsters chased the stinky smells around and around the Hall of Freaks, leaving a path of destruction behind them. At first, they seemed interested in the scents, but then as soon as they got up close for a good sniff, they turned away again. Molly couldn't figure out what monsters usually liked to eat, and she was eager to find something that would hold their attention for more than a few seconds.

The museum was absolute chaos—stuffed beasts toppled over, props were thrown this way and that, and the scents that now filled the room were absolutely putrid. Rotten meat and garlic and dirt and the odor of foul monster breath all combined into one awful bouquet. Penelope knew there was no way she was going to calm herself until the monsters settled down and gave her a minute to just breathe.

"The class is going outside," Cork said, staring at the wall with a look of great concentration. Penelope watched him warily as she tried to calm herself. She couldn't understand how a pair of cheap plastic glasses could actually *work* to see through things, but it seemed like Cork was confident about what was happening on the other side of the walls. Uncle Cork chuckled and said, "Finn is an interesting kid, i'nt he?"

A moment later, Finn burst through the archway leading into the Hall of Freaks. He was hugging the blue sensory box that Tom had told them was filled with eyeballs. "I found Mr. Intihar and the fourth graders by the sensory boxes, just like you said, Uncle Cork! And that's when I had my in peck a bull idea!"

CHAPTER 16

Eyes on My Fingers

The monsters both turned and gaped at Finn, drool oozing from their mouths. Bree, Cork, Molly, and Penelope all stared at him, too. Gramps was—incredibly—*still* snoozing. Bree rushed over to protect her son from the spooks, who were now looking at Finn the same way many people might eye a piece of fudge.

Finn pried open the top of the sensory box and popped each of his skinny fingers into the hole of an olive. Then he began to sing a little song. "I've got eyes on my fingers . . ." He held several olive-covered fingers up against his forehead and sang, "I've got eyes on my forehead." He sashayed and danced around the room, dropping olives in a little trail as he dashed through the Hall of Freaks.

For the first time since they'd burst through the closet doors, the monsters looked almost calm. As if in a daze, they followed Finn around like he was their master. Trancelike, the monsters walked side by side, gobbling up olives just as quickly as Finn could lay them down. With each bite, the monsters grew more and more calm—until eventually, they each sat down on the floor beside the two Creep Closets and chewed on their snacks.

"Olives!" Molly marveled. "Of course."

"I don't get it," said Uncle Cork.

153

"Olives are Niblet's favorite snack," explained Pen.

"I was wondering if they might be *every* monster's favorite snack," Finn replied cheerfully. "I had an idea about the eyeballs. I'm a very bright boy."

"You are a very bright boy indeed," agreed Cork.

The monsters chewed and swallowed, getting their fill of olives. After several long minutes

of peace and quiet while the monsters snacked, both of the spooks began to grow more and more still. It was almost as though they were turning into statues, right before the Quirks' very eyes.

"They're very quiet," mused Uncle Cork.

"I feel better," agreed Penelope.

"Problem solved," cheered Finn. "Thanks to Finnegan Quirk. Hooray that I'm here!"

"Just because you had one good idea, don't go thinking you're excused for your actions today, young man," scolded Bree. "This morning's she-nanigans were a *very* bad idea. If I were you, I'd eat up all of the food you can find here at the museum, because it's going to be a week of your very least favorite meals at home."

155

Molly had a hard time keeping a straight face.

Suddenly, Cork burst out laughing, too.

"What's funny?" asked Pen.

Cork continued to laugh. He pointed at his forehead, then at the X-ray glasses that he was still wearing.

"The glasses?" wondered Molly. "What's so funny about the glasses?"

Cork giggled and snorted, unable to control himself. "Finn . . . ," he finally managed. "He had an eye on his forehead."

"It was an olive," Molly said, not comprehending why that was so funny. She hadn't found Finn's little dance particularly hilarious. She couldn't understand why it was cracking her uncle up so much. "Olives on his fingers and his forehead."

"It was an eye." Cork giggled.

Now Bree, too, was laughing.

"Seriously," Penelope said, annoyed. "*That* is cracking you up? Mom, no offense, but you've been a crab all week . . . Finn's olive dance is the thing that's going to make you cheerful again?"

Bree snorted.

"It's just . . . ," Cork said, teary. "It's just that . . ." He pulled off the X-ray glasses and tossed them on the floor. He looked at Bree. After a long moment, she nodded. "These glasses don't actually work. They're just a toy, you know."

"But they worked for you," Finn said. "You said so yourself. You could see the class through the wall, by the sensory boxes. And you were right. That's exactly where they were."

"That had nothing to do with these glasses," Cork said, more seriously now. "And everything to do with this."

Slowly, Uncle Cork raised his hat off his head. Then, a centimeter at a time, he lifted his rainbow sweatband up, up, up. There, smack dab in the middle of Uncle Cork's forehead, was a very small eye. All three Quirk kids gasped.

"You've got an eye on your forehead!" Finn announced.

"That I do," agreed Cork. "It's my extra eye."

"You have an extra eye?" asked Finn, even though it was very, *very* obvious that the answer was, in fact, yes. "What's that about?"

"This is my Quirk," said Cork simply. "I was born with an extra eye. This one is special, though. I can see through things, and it comes in particularly handy for spotting mischief and mayhem."

"You can see *through* stuff?" Finn asked. "That is *so* unfair."

"You're invisible!" Cork shot back. "I'd argue that that is also unfair and very, very cool."

Pen cocked her head at her uncle. "So . . . you have X-ray vision?"

"I guess you could call it whatever strikes your fancy. I just call it my bonus eye. My extra-strong sense of sight. I can't see through skin or anything creepy like that, but I can see through walls and other solid objects. It's almost as if all walls and boxes and doors are made of glass when I look at them. Also, my extra eye can see Finn, even when he's invisible. That's a neat perk."

Molly closed her eyes. "Of course! You told us some of your senses are more refined than ours. You have a super-duper sense of sight."

"Right-o." Cork smiled. Then he took a deep breath and said, "When you kids were all so curious about my Quirk, I figured it might be fun to keep it a secret from you for a while. See, there aren't many people in my life who don't know about it, so it was kind of nice to live under an air of mystery for the last few days."

"Unfair . . . ," muttered Finn.

"Hold on," said Molly. "What do you mean, there aren't many people who don't know about it?"

Cork glanced at Bree again. Without waiting for her permission, he blurted out, "I don't keep my Quirk hidden, the way you do here. I've long been honest about my Quirks back home, and the folks in my neighborhood know all about my differences now."

159

"They know?" murmured Penelope, looking up at him. Quietly, she asked, "And they don't care?"

"When I first tell people about it, they look at me a bit strangely, sure," said Cork. "But after too many years of hiding my Quirk, I was fed up with never getting to be myself. Over time, I've learned that once I get to know people and tell them about my special feature, my Quirk doesn't seem to bother them.

They realize we're really the same, deep down—it's just that my Quirks are a little more obvious."

"A little?" blurted Finn. "A lot! You have a third eye!"

"True," said Cork. "But I made the choice long ago to not live my life in fear. I picked a town where I knew people are open and welcoming, and I've just been honest about who I am."

Bree finally spoke up. "It's worked for Cork, but that doesn't mean it would work for us. Things are different here. Everyone is very similar to each other in Normal, and if they knew how different we were, well . . ."

Molly and Penelope both nodded. Penelope looked sad, but resigned to their reality.

"We know," said Molly. "It's just really lucky that Cork gets to tell people about his Quirk. If Pen could tell people about her magic, she wouldn't have to worry about it acting up all the time. If she wasn't always so concerned about it getting her into trouble, maybe she'd stop freaking out."

"I don't freak out," Pen said sullenly. Then she looked at the monsters, and at the mess that filled the Hall of Freaks, and at the scent packets that littered the floor. She also thought about all the times her imagination had gotten worked up in school, and how—when she'd tried to squish her magical mind down—it always seemed to make everything worse. "Okay, so maybe I sometimes freak out. But it's just because I get so nervous about people finding out about us. If people *knew* . . ." She quietly trailed off.

"Now is not the time to talk about this," said Cork, tense again. "The class is comin' back this way."

"Our monsters!" said Molly. "We need to make sure our monsters are as they were when the class left." The teams' monsters were quiet and still again, but looked much messier than they had when the class had left the Hall of Freaks. She and Pen quickly walked over and tried to clean them up as much as possible. They reattached limbs that had gotten loose during the scuffle, and made sure the fur and skin were put back in place.

Penelope also made a few adjustments to her team's monster that she hoped would help it be a bit more steady on its feet. After seeing how wobbly it was when it had come to life,

she knew they'd made the ogre head too large for its skinny body. She also considered what Tom and Christine had said about alerting all five senses, and hastily tucked a sound chip into the creature's shirt. Now, whenever someone came near, the witchy ogre burped. Penelope also opened one of the raw onion scent packets and dumped the contents across its shoulders. It looked, smelled, sounded, felt, and probably also—if anyone was brave enough to find out— *tasted* disgusting.

While the girls put their monsters back together, Cork, Bree, and Finn cleaned up as much as they were able to around the Hall of Freaks. Finn reminded them of what Tom had said earlier in the day. "'Member? He said not to worry about messes—they said they can clean it all up later."

"I'm not sure this is quite what he had in mind," said Cork, gazing around at the overturned displays and scattered props and clothing. "Ah, well. Bree, I suspect the kids' questions won't really be an issue, but could you do us a bitty favor and let Christine and Tom know they ought not worry about either the mess or how it got here?"

Bree took a deep breath and said, "I think I should be able to manage that. Then Finn and I need to skedaddle. Someone"—she glanced at Finn—"has overstayed his welcome."

"Penelope? You all set?" Cork glanced at the wall. Now they all knew he was looking *through* it, which was really neat. "The class is almost here."

Pen took a deep breath and gave her monster one last look. With her chin held high, she said, "I'm ready. No more monsters coming alive today." She tapped her head and said, "This time I'm all set. Imagination managed."

Before the class stormed back into the Hall of Freaks, Molly looked from her team's hairy, one-eyed monster to the witchy ogre her sister's team had created. She had to admit that Pen's team's creation was quite a bit creepier than her own. She studied the ogre creature's detailed face and scratchy fingernails, and got a whiff of the onion scent Pen had added at the last minute. When Penelope walked toward the beast and it burped, Molly realized the other team's spook was totally grotesque and the obvious winner.

Her team's creature was still sort of comical. Molly glanced at her own spook again, trying to figure out if there was something they could do to beat the other group in the challenge. And that's when she noticed something. Under the long matted fur and the olive spots . . . her creature was now wearing a pair of pink-and-yellow underwear.

And the Winner Is . . .

CHAPTER 17

At first, most of the kids in the fourth-grade class didn't really notice that anything in the Hall of Freaks was amiss. In all their years of trying to hide their differences, the Quirks had found that unless something directly impacted someone, most people were usually fairly oblivious to strange things happening around them. Fortunately, that's exactly what happened at Spook City that day.

There were a few questions about what Molly and Penelope had been doing in the Hall of Freaks while the rest of the group was out in the lobby and exploring the rest of the museum a second time. Those questions were easily explained away by Finn's presence and the girls' need to help their mother get him ready to go. Bree dealt with the adults, doling out a bit of her Quirky magic, and soon all was nearly forgotten amidst the excitement of wrapping up the competition.

After several minutes, the groups were back at work on their monsters' finishing touches. "Who put our monster in underwear?" Stella demanded. "Raade? Was that you? It's really immature."

Across the room, Molly could hear her sister giggling quietly.

Shortly after Bree, Finn, and Martha had left the museum, Tom and Christine called time. "We're ready to judge your creations. It's time to determine our winner in today's Normal Elementary School Spook Style team challenge," Christine announced. "Please finish up any final details, and then step away from your monsters."

The teams scurried around their creatures, trying to make sure there was enough fake blood and torn fur and rotten flesh before it was too late

to change anything more. Then the contest was over—and judging began.

Christine and Tom both walked slowly around each of the creatures, investigating them from head to paw. Christine smiled slightly when she sniffed Penelope's team's monster, and when it burped Tom looked startled at first and then he began to laugh. Though the ogre-like head was still too large for the extremely thin body, Penelope had done a good job of shoring it up so it stood still and tall for the judges.

Everyone waited, eager for the guides to choose a winner. When he couldn't stand the suspense any longer, Nolan blurted out, "The ogre head was my idea! If you like it, just know that's all me."

Christine arched an eyebrow at him, but said nothing.

Grandpa Quill woke up just as Tom and Christine finished inspecting his team's creation. "What did I miss?" he asked, bleary. He yawned, then rubbed his belly. "I'm starving. Somethin' smells like fried onions . . . A burger would taste great right about now."

The judges moved to the other creature. They studied its fur, the oozing eye, the stubby arms, and its olive-colored spots. "This one smells like olives," murmured Tom. "I didn't know we had olive scent packets. I must say, that's an . . . *interesting* choice."

Cork smiled at Molly and Penelope.

"You know, I think I have my winner picked," said Tom, after what felt like an eternity. "How about you, Christine?"

"I do." Christine rubbed her fingers over the skull necklace around her neck. "I certainly do."

They whispered to each other for a moment, then Tom nodded. "We are ready to announce our choice."

Mr. Intihar shushed the kids. They began to crowd forward around Tom and Christine, waiting for the results. Even Cork and Grandpa Quill looked on eagerly.

Finally, Tom said, "The winner of today's Spook Style team challenge is . . ." His head swung left to eye Pen's team's creation, then swiveled right to look at Molly's team's creation. ". . . the onion ogre! Congratulations to Christine's team, who has won the competition."

Penelope, Norah, Joey, Nolan, and the others on Christine and Grandpa Quill's team jumped up and down in the Hall of Freaks. In his enthusiasm, Nolan knocked their ogre over onto the floor. Its head popped right off and rolled across the room. "Oops." He shrugged, then scrambled to grab it and put it back in its place.

Tom quieted the class down. "The reason we selected this team's creation is that they really tickled all of our senses with their attention to

171

detail. The onion smell, the clever combination of elements in the costuming and design, the sharp fingernails, and—of course—that horrible belch all combined into one awful beast. Whoever thought to add the sound chip, that was pure genius. The addition of that final sensory element took your creature from ordinary to extraordinary."

Penelope beamed. Though she would never brag about her contribution to her team, she felt proud knowing that she had been the one to add the sound chip to their creation at the last minute. She also knew that if she hadn't battled Nolan at the beginning of their challenge, she probably wouldn't have been comfortable adding her ideas to what would have been Nolan's monster. She was glad they'd worked together as a team to come up with a group design they could all feel proud of.

"Congratulations, kids," said Mr. Intihar, high-fiving the winning group. "I guess this means you'll be joining the Spook City folks at their haunted house. You'll be behind the scenes, scaring the people of Normal!"

The kids on Uncle Cork's team looked crushed.

"Don't look so sad," said Christine softly. "We know how hard you worked on your creature, and we don't want you to leave here empty-handed."

"Does everyone win?" asked Stella. "We get to be in the haunted house, too?"

"No," said Christine sharply. "I don't believe in the everyone-wins philosophy. People need to learn how to be gracious losers."

"So . . . what gives?" asked Raade. "Do we get a gift bag with some spider rings or something?"

"You get to go home knowing your experiences today have given you a fun behind-the-scenes peek at a haunted house," said Tom. "Which will come in handy when . . ." He trailed off.

Christine continued. "When you visit us as our guests at the haunted house tomorrow night. We're giving you all passes to the Spook City Haunted House, so that your winning classmates will have the opportunity to scare *you*, too."

Molly and the others in Uncle Cork's group cheered.

173

Tom went on. "Though you won't get to be a part of the haunted house, you will get to visit for free." He passed purple tickets to everyone on Molly's team. "This is our way of saying thanks for creating one of the creatures that will be featured in the Spook City Haunted House on Halloween night."

"What do you mean?" asked Molly. "You're using our monster in your haunted house?"

"If it's okay with you," Christine said. "We need to fill the haunted house kitchen with all kinds of characters, cooking up mounds of gross food. We'd love to use the spooks your groups have created today as characters in our creepy cafeteria. They look great, and it would be a shame to see these beautiful beasts go to waste."

Stella beamed. "It's definitely okay with us."

"Well, class," said Mr. Intihar, glancing down at his watch, "we need to hop on the bus and get you back to school. Tom, Christine: thank you for everything today. I'm sure I speak for everyone when I say we've had a great time and learned a lot."

"You're very welcome," said Tom, bowing. "We'd love to have you all come back to visit us again next year. For those of you who will be helping out in the haunted house tomorrow night, please report for a costume check and makeup at four o'clock. The rest of you are invited at five

174

for the grand opening of this year's Spook City Haunted House."

As the students from room six walked out of the Hall of Freaks for the last time, Molly and Penelope glanced back for one final look at their teams' Spook Style creations. When they did, Molly was pretty sure she saw Pen's ogre-witch lift its hand in a tiny wave. Then the creature released one last, loud burp to say good-bye.

CHAPTER 18

An Ill-fitting Mask

At home that night, none of the Quirks could stop talking about how much fun they'd had at Spook City. Gran and Bree were both busily asking questions about the museum while they enjoyed their meal of tofu and broccoli stir-fry out on the deck.

As added punishment for his field trip shenanigans that day, Finn wasn't allowed to talk about Spook City or the Spook Style team challenge or any of the Quirky mishaps that had happened until his plate was empty. In the fifteen minutes they had been sitting at the table, he'd only managed a tiny bite off a single piece of tofu, and was now building a grove of trees out of the broccoli.

While Finn fiddled, Molly and Penelope told all the fun highlights of the day. They shared stories from the Spook Style challenge, talked all about the different rooms in the museum, and told their mom and Gran about the Haunted House the next night.

"Are you worried about being a part of the haunted house, Penelope?" asked Bree, her face lined with worry. "I know how situations like that can be difficult for you."

"Well, I was a little nervous about it at first, but I think I'm going to be okay," Pen said. "Being a part of the haunted house will be a lot easier than walking through it as a regular person, actually. I'll get to be behind the scenes, so there won't be any real surprises for me to worry about."

"I would also be happy to help out, if you wanted me to," said Uncle Cork. "I can take a peek and let you know what's hiding around all the corners and doors and such. There's not much that can surprise me, with this guy along for the ride." He tapped his forehead.

177

"That would be great," Pen said. Then she glanced at Gran. "Oh, and in case you were wondering, we also finally found out about Uncle Cork's Quirk today. It sure did come in handy for keeping an extra eye on Finn at the museum."

"Hmmmpf," grumbled Finn, stabbing a piece of broccoli with his fork. Then, quietly, he slid a chunk of tofu off his plate and dropped it on the ground for Pickles. The dat dashed over to sniff the treat, then put up her little nose and trotted away without even a tiny taste. "Even dats don't like tofu," Finn pointed out. "This punishment is the pits."

"Cork's Quirk certainly was a wee challenge when he was small," said Gran, her tinkling laughter carrying merrily through the backyard. "Fortunately, your mother's powers were already strong enough when she was young that she was able to sort things out at the hospital where Cork was born. Took a mighty lot of convincing to get people to forget about a newborn with an extra eye, but it all worked out in the end."

"When did you start telling people about your magic?" Molly asked Cork.

Bree's mouth was set into a thin line. She'd been so joyful earlier in the day that the girls had hoped maybe some of the awkwardness with Cork had passed. Apparently, they were wrong.

Cork relaxed back into one of the Adirondack chairs out on the deck and began to talk. "When we were kids, Bree—your mother—and I used to play with our Quirks all the time. I'd spy on her, and tell Mum when she was makin' mischief—or messes—with her friends. She could never hide anything from me. And my sister? She hated that I used my Quirk against her."

Glaring at him, Bree nodded. Both Molly and Penelope knew how terrible it would feel to have someone spying on you inside the safety of your own home all the time. They'd all witnessed this firsthand with Mrs. DeVille!

As a twin, it sometimes felt as if it was impossible to do anything alone. But because they'd always had each other, Molly and Pen kind of liked having a partner for most things. Their mother, however, was the kind of person who guarded her privacy dearly. Molly wondered if this was a trait she'd been born with, or if it had developed because of

179

Cork's snooping when they were younger. The girls realized Cork's snooping was probably part of the reason Bree and her brother had grown apart.

Cork chuckled and went on. "To get back at me, Bree would make me do all sorts of things I didn't want to do: wear silly-looking tucked-in shirts with preppy belts to school, clean her room when she was supposed to be doin' it. And worst of all, she used her magic to force me to keep my extra eye covered all the time."

"Of course I made you keep your eye covered all the time!" Bree interrupted. "You were always trying to tell people about our magic, and I had no interest in having people stare at us in town."

Cork blinked. "We're two very different people, your mother and I," he said finally. "I don't much care if people stare, but it's always bothered her."

Bree's nostrils flared. "You make it sound very simple," she said. "You make it sound as if I'm not proud of the person I am, or of the family we are. But I am. I'm very proud to be a Quirk. I just want to ensure that my children have the easiest life they can have, filled with privacy and respect from others, if that's what they choose. If this means we need to hide our magic from the outside world and move from time to time to keep people from prying, well, so be it. It's a choice I've made, and I don't appreciate you making my children think that sharing their Quirks with the world would be easy. Because it's not."

No one said anything for a long time. The girls looked from their mother, to Cork, to Gran and Grandpa, who were sharing the other Adirondack chair. Even Pickles and Finn were silent, curled up on the deck.

Finally, it was Penelope who spoke. "Sometimes . . ." She swallowed, then looked to Molly for support. She and Molly had talked about what it would be like if they told people about the family's Quirks many times. They'd considered telling people about their differences, but each time, one of the girls had talked the other out of it.

Mostly, because as a pair of just-turned-ten-year-olds who were frequently deposited into new classes in new schools in new towns, they understood how hard it was to be different and strange and new. They had experienced what it was like to be the kind of people who struggled to feel like they fit in. If people knew about their secrets, it would be impossible to even *pretend* to be like everyone else. They'd learned to love their differences, but shouting about them to the world had always seemed too frightening.

"Sometimes," Pen said quietly again, "I do wish I could tell people about my Quirks. Our magic is a part of who we are, and I wish more people could know me for me. I hate being scared to show my friends who I really am."

"Oh, Pen." Bree sighed. It was impossible to tell what their mother was feeling, as her expression was unfamiliar.

"I do, Mom," continued Penelope, her voice strong and sure. "And it's not just because of Uncle Cork, either. It's that I spend so much effort trying to hide my magic, and the thing is . . . everything is always worse for us when we're worried about someone finding out our secrets. Maybe it wouldn't be as bad as we think, if we could just be honest about who we are and how we're different."

"Look at Mrs. DeVille," said Molly, glancing over at the fence along the side yard. "She found out about Gran, and it was really no big deal once she got used to the idea of having a teensy friend. Don't you ever wonder what it might be like if we let people get to know the *real* us, rather than moving every time one of us slips up?"

Bree looked as if she was close to tears. The girls knew their mother was always trying to protect them by keeping them sheltered and hidden. But sometimes her protection went a bit too far. Sometimes she held on too tightly, and it hurt instead of helped.

That day, the girls began to wonder: At what point were they old enough to decide how they wanted the world to see them? Pen had been growing tired of always trying to be someone else. It was like she put on a Halloween costume every day. When, she wondered, would she be allowed to take off her very ordinary and ill-fitting mask and expose her true self?

"This isn't a matter that's up for discussion," said Bree, her voice slipping.

"Now, Bree," urged Grandpa Quill. There were very few times when Gramps acted much like a father to his daughter, as he was often too busy making mischief of his own to be much of a role model. But it was suddenly clear from his tone of voice that he was about to offer some fatherly advice. "We've supported your choice to remain quiet all these years. Your mother and I have been here to help you as you raise these wonderful kids. And all this time, we've done things your way. But I think you should consider letting the children figure out who they are as individuals."

The girls watched their mother sigh, a full-body gasp that left her body sunken and shaky. "I knew this would happen if you came to visit," Bree said finally, looking at Cork. The girls realized now that their mom hadn't been *mad* at Cork, as they'd thought—she had been worried. Nervous he'd let the cat out of the bag about his own way of dealing with Quirks, and might somehow ruin things for the Normal side of his family.

"Don' blame me, Bree," said Cork softly. "We all need to live our own lives, and your girls were bound to realize that everyone makes different choices that suit them at some point in life. Just as I did. And just as you have."

"I'm sorry," Bree said, after many long seconds. She looked at Cork, her eyes wide and unblinking.

"I'm sorry I made you hide who you were all those years when we were kids. You're right. It wasn't my life to live, and it wasn't my choice to make. For that, I apologize."

Cork stood and clumsily picked up his sister. He spun her in his arms, then plunked her down and gave her a kiss. "Aw, I forgave you years ago, Bree-tie. I gave you your fair share of hassle, too. You're not the only one to blame."

"And you," Bree said, turning to Penelope. "If telling people about your magic is something you'd like to do, well . . ." She closed her eyes. "Well, sweetheart, you're old enough to make smart choices. We'll just need to discuss it a bit more as a family, and then figure out how to come clean. It could get messy, but I'm willing to try."

"Really?" said Pen, her eyes wide. "No more secrets? No more hiding? I could just be . . . me?"

Bree nodded resolutely. "Really." She looked at Gran and Gramps, who smiled back at her as if they'd been waiting for her to come around to this decision for many years. "And if everyone else wants to come clean, too. Well. I'm willing to be a part of that."

Molly held Finn's shoulder, even while Pickles clamored for her share of the family's attention. Penelope grinned, looking as relaxed and happy as Molly had ever seen her. Bree brushed back her hair and finished, "Because you know what I think? I think Normal is as good a place as any for us to try to be ourselves."

CHAPTER 19

SPOOK HOUSE

Well, well, *well*.

There had been some mighty big decisions made at the Quirk house on the Friday before All Hallows' Eve. When the family awoke on Halloween morning—roused, as usual, by the sound of Cork snoring—everyone had some doubts about their new plan. These doubts had crawled into the curvy spaces in their brains overnight, and now they were slinking around demanding attention.

Gramps was the first to speak of their conversation from the night before. "We-*elll*," he said at breakfast. He'd made his famous Halloween eggballs—hard-boiled eggs made to look like eyeballs, with a bacon mustache and a ketchup mouth. There was also a bowl of candy corn on the table that not one single Quirk could resist. "We're comin' clean, eh?"

"Sounds like it," agreed Molly.

"Today?" wondered Finn.

"Tomorrow." Penelope strode into the kitchen confidently. "After Halloween. Today is a day for masks and costumes. Tomorrow, though, it all comes off. Tomorrow is the first day of a whole new life for these Quirks. A day without masks or makeup or costumes—a day to let everyone know what we're like without our disguises."

Their mother slid into a seat at the kitchen table and nodded. "I see you haven't changed your mind overnight."

"Not one bit," declared Penelope.

The others tucked into their eggs. For the first time in a long while, the kitchen was full of Quirks . . . and totally silent.

As the day wore on, Molly grew more and more nervous about the next day's big reveal. But luckily, she, Penelope, and Finn had Halloween costumes to prepare—and the Spook City Haunted House to look forward to. She and Penelope worked on their costumes all day. Each girl had decided to use some of the techniques they'd learned the previous day at the museum to make a spooky costume to wear that night. Penelope knew she needed to be as scary as possible, considering the fact that she was going to be part of the haunted house.

The girls giggled and sewed and shredded all day, until they both had costumes they were proud of. Penelope resembled the Wicked Witch of the West from *The Wizard of Oz*—but she was planning to wait to paint her face green until she got to Spook City later that afternoon. Molly was a cross between a scarecrow and a zombie, with torn-up clothes and a dirty face that Gran helped her scuff up out in the garden. Finn insisted he was going to wear underwear and a cape, and that was all.

"You said we could be ourselves!" insisted Finn, when Bree protested. "What's wrong with undies?"

"Not hiding our Quirks is one thing . . . not hiding our underwear is another thing altogether," Bree said, laughing. Eventually, Cork wrapped Finn in two small sheep rugs he dug out of the depths of his massive suitcase. Finn loved them, and called himself Superhero Sheep.

Even Niblet and Pickles got in on the Halloween action. First Niblet poked out of the girls' bedroom door, his legs and arms stuffed into Gramps's clothes and suspenders. Cork's hat was perched atop the monster's head, and the girls decided he looked like a fuzzy Scottish Highlander.

Later, Niblet and Finn forced Pickles into a tiny pig costume that she scratched at desperately as though she were embarrassed. The little dat spun around and around in circles, chasing the curlicue pigtail until she collapsed in a frustrated heap right in the middle of the front hall.

"My very own potbellied piggy!" squealed Finn, chasing Pickles around the house joyfully. After a long game of chase, Pickles finally managed to shed most of her costume, but couldn't get the piggy tail off her backside no matter how hard she tried.

"Are we ready to head out?" Cork asked late in the afternoon after everyone was finished with costumes. Cork, Bree, and Grandpa Quill had put together costumes as well, and they were dressed as the Tin Man, Dorothy, and the Cowardly Lion from *The Wizard of Oz*. Gran had even gotten in on the action, and looked like a small and lovely version of Glinda the Good Witch. She was adorable.

Molly realized she had sort of made herself into a creepy version of the Scarecrow. Pickles was a lot like Toto, and Niblet reminded her of a Munchkin. And Finn? Well, Finn did kind of resemble one of the Wicked Witch's flying monkeys. They hadn't planned it, but the Quirks were really rocking a theme.

As the family gathered in the front hall preparing to go, the doorbell rang. Outside, Mr. Intihar and his son, Charlie, stood on the front porch. Charlie was dressed in a Tootsie Roll costume, and Mr. Intihar was wearing a full four-piece suit and tie, complete with an enormous top hat.

Everyone piled into the Quirks' van and drove out to Spook City together.

Penelope dashed inside the museum as soon as they arrived to finish getting ready and find out what her job would be inside the haunted house. Meanwhile, the others sat on the grass outside and listened to Cork's stories about his hometown. Bree laughed along with everyone else, and Molly felt good knowing her mom had come to realize how great her brother was during his visit. She wasn't ready for Uncle Cork to leave and really hoped they'd be able to see him again soon.

When Pen got inside the museum, she could see that the staff had worked overnight to turn the whole place into an incredible haunted house. They had taken down most of the exhibits and displays and turned the place into a full-fledged spookville. Penelope was relieved everyone was getting things set up for the grand opening—that meant the lights had been left on.

She took in all the gross displays, and trick coffins, and tried to imagine what it would be like when all the lights went out and she was part of the group responsible for scaring all her neighbors, friends, classmates, and family. She grinned. This was going to be great! Uncle Cork was planning to join her later, just in case. Her uncle, combined with her lights-on sneak peek, made Pen feel confident that she'd be able to enjoy a haunted house for the first time in her entire life.

Penelope wandered around aimlessly for a few minutes before she found Norah and Nolan, both digging through the prop closets they'd used the day before while designing their creeps. They were both pawing through boxes of supplies, and they— along with the other members of their team—were giggling madly as they accessorized their costumes with professional extras. Tom and Christine were both on hand, too, dashing here and there to add a little of this to Norah's ghost costume and a little of that to Nolan's ogre. Christine offered to help Penelope paint her skin green, and before long, it was time for everyone to take their places inside the haunted house.

Together with the rest of her team, Pen trailed behind Tom and Christine as they assigned every- one to a station. Nolan was supposed to lie inside a coffin, then pop up when people walked by.

Joey was going to be working alongside Tom in one of the rooms that had been made to look like an old, moldy dining room. Pen and Norah were both assigned to help out in the room that had been turned into a kitchen. They would be offering up platters of oozing eyeballs and worm soup to guests who came through.

When the gleaming overhead lights were on inside the kitchen, it was kind of a funny scene. But as soon as the lights went out and the whole room was awash in blue light, the Spook City kitchen had a very ominous feel. Pen and Norah had a blast trying out different voices and faces while they waited for their families to walk through.

The moment the lights went out and they were "on," Penelope realized she wasn't going to need Uncle Cork's help getting through the haunted house after all. Now that she'd made the decision to tell people about her Quirk the very next day, she was much less worried about any strange things that could happen because of her magical mind. It was a part of her, and whatever happened, happened.

195

As Pen dished up platters of steaming worms and cackled at the people who walked by her, she thought about the new life that was about to begin for the Quirks. If Uncle Cork had survived—and thrived!—all these years without keeping quiet about his magic, well, she would be just fine, too. They all would.

When Molly and Finn and the rest of the family came through the kitchen a short while later, Pen was ready for them. Focusing on her cauldron of soup, Penelope made the pot glow and ooze. Staring into the murky brown broth (really just beef stock and noodles), Pen thought: *Worms. Let's see some real, ooey-gooey worms.*

Finn flapped his cape, chomped his gum, and reached his little hand inside the pot for a feel. He snatched it back out immediately. "Those are real worms!" he screeched. "I was hoping for chocolate or something funny. You booby-trapped me!"

Molly laughed, peeked inside the pot, and murmured, "Nicely done, Pen." She and her sister shared a sly smile. Then Molly added, "I can't wait for more people to see what you can do."

Uncle Cork lifted one eyebrow and leaned in close to Molly and Penelope. "Even though I'm going back to Scotland tomorrow morning, you should both know I'll be keeping an extra eye on you from afar." He winked and tipped his tin cap. "And all I can say is, the world better watch out for the Quirks. The town of Normal has no idea what's in store for them."

Penelope tipped her head back and cackled again, all the while staying in character. As she watched her family move on to the next room, Pen thought about how she only had a few hours left of pretending to be someone else, and then it would all be over—the secrets, the hiding, the lies. As much as she loved wearing disguises, Pen couldn't wait to see what it would feel like tomorrow when all the masks and costumes were gone.

Tomorrow morning, their family would step out the front door, skip down the crumbling front steps, and traipse past their ham-scented fence. Then they would finally get to show the world how fabulous it was to be a Quirk.